BIG BANG

Ron Goulart

DAW BOOKS, INC.
DONALD A. WOLLHEIM, PUBLISHER

1633 Broadway, New York, NY 10019

FIRST PRINTING, JULY 1982

1 2 3 4 5 6 7 8 9

DAW TRADEMARK REGISTERED
U.S. PAT. OFF. MARCA
REGISTRADA. HECHO EN U.S.A.

PRINTED IN U.S.A.

Hildy was angry. "Jake Pace, the next time you commit a brutal sex crime, I'll let you rot."

"Rot? Rotting I could handle," Jake said. "But when you are convicted of a sex crime in this part of the country they rehabilitate you. Rehabilitation in America's Heartland means being taken out of the sexual competition permanently. Not only that, they also fix you so you don't even think about ladies or gents or whatever the opposite sex may be for you. They even fix your brain so you start having doubts about the theory of evolution."

Hildy patted his hand. "I wouldn't want you not to be able to think about Darwin once in a while," she said. "You have so little fun in life as it is. If it weren't for going to bed with blonde sopranos behind my back every so often you'd. . . ."

CHAPTER 1

The rat he'd been watching fell over.

Jake Pace blinked, swallowed twice and made another try at getting himself oriented. He was a long, lean man of thirty-six, tanned, and handsome in a grim sort of way. Right at the moment he was sprawled, front-down, on a grey stone floor with his head near what might be the leg of an old-fashioned sofa.

From out of the rathole in the bleak stone wall that was some seven or eight feet from him another rat, timidly, peered.

Zzzzzzummmmmmmm!

A stungun hummed somewhere beyond Jake's present range of vision.

"Chip!" said the rat and toppled over, stiff, beside its mate.

"That's about enough of this particular sport," Jake attempted to say. But only a gargly groan came out.

"Heck now! Are you sure enough awake?" inquired a slightly tinny voice. "I was just simply stunnin' a few rats to pass the time whiles waitin' for you to recover some, Mr. Pack."

"It's Pace," Jake managed to mumble. Pushing hard at the chill stone floor with both hands, he raised his torso.

5

"Here now, lemme help you, sir." A rocking chair twanged, metallic feet clomped on stone.

Then a warm metal hand slid into his armpit and tugged Jake up into a sitting position. "Thanks," he said.

"It's my job after all, Mr. Pace. Got 'er right that time. Pace." Grinning down at him was a large, ball-headed robot. He was copper-plated and decked out in a pair of spotless white bib overalls. "My name's Shux-2036 an' if you need any darn thing durin' your stay with us, why you just—"

"Where is it I'm supposed to be staying?" Immediately next to him was a soft, comfortable-looking sofa. A pretty fair imitation of an early 20th century piece. "I was at . . ." He paused, shook his head and had the sudden impression the sofa went sliding into the stone wall.

The robot chuckled, then said, " 'Scuse me for laughin' at your discomfort, sir. Thing is, though, seein' somebody comin' to after bein' stungunned is always sort of funny."

Noticing the stunrod cradled in the mechanism's arm, Jake inquired, "Did you—"

"Heck no. I ain't allowed to hurt none of you inmates. We go strictly by robotics rules here. No, sir, I . . . 'scuse me"

Zummmmmmm!

Shux had paused to use his rod on a new rat who'd emerged.

Jake clutched at the arm of the sofa, got himself up and seated on one of its flowered cuchions. "I can't seem to recall exactly why I'm—"

"Rats ain't the same."

"Hum?"

"As people." The robot lowered his silvery stunrod, settled back into the rocker facing Jake. "Case you might be wonderin' how come, after me tellin' you I weren't allowed to hurt folks here, I could shoot rats with impunity. Reason for that is, rats ain't people. That's basic robotics procedure."

The room was about twenty feet square, the walls of real stone. There were no doors visible in the walls, not a single window or viewhole. Besides the sofa and the rocking chair the room contained, in one corner, an unshielded toilet and some sort of low platform about twice the diameter of the privy.

"Suppose, Shux, you get back to filling me in on where it is I find myself," suggested Jake. "After that I'd like to make arrangements to depart from this—"

"Doggone! You sure do got a sense of humor." The robot slapped an overalled knee and produced a clanging sound. "You ain't goin' to get out of here for weeks an' weeks."

"Why? Am I sick or. . . ."

"This is Murderers Home," explained Shux. "And the reason you're here, Mr. Pace, sir, is 'cause you're a murderer. Alleged murderer, they make us say. Now, soon's they run all the prelim tests on you, then you'll have a hearin' an'—"

"What the hell are you talking about?" Jake stood up and the dizziness caught him again. He closed his eyes, sitting. "I'm Jake Pace. My wife and I run Odd Jobs, Inc. one of the top private inquiry agencies in the—"

"Ain't that a darn shame. Here you got a wife, pretty one I just bet, an' yet you get to foolin' around with floozies an'—"

"Where is my wife?" Jake thought to ask. "Has she been notif—"

"Oh, surely, don't you fret. Mr. Benton knows exact how to process a murderer so as—"

"Whoa now." Jake opened his eyes to stare at his

mechanical guard. "Are you perhaps alluding to Bullet Benton of the Federal Police Agency? What has that goon got to—"

"Mr. Benton apprehended you, sir," replied Shux. "You are dang lucky you got yourself caught by a man of his caliber. He got you booked into one of the best way stations for murderers in all of America. Otherwise, they maybe would've tossed you into Death Row up Detroit ways or—"

"Just why did Bullet Benton apprehend me?"

"'Cause you killed that poor girl is why." The robot leaned forward in his rocker. "Don't you honest remember doin' it?"

Jake concentrated, distracted some by the sudden loud gurgling of his toilet. "I was . . . No, Hildy and I were in our place in Connecticut," he said, mostly to himself. "A pixphone call came in . . . a client . . . no, somebody . . . somebody wanted to see me about. . . ." He straightened up. "What time is it?"

"Shade past eight AM Omaha Heartland Time," replied Shux. "The date, case you need that, is Tuesday, December 23. If that FPA stungun really knocked you silly, I better mention the year is 2003. Real shame you murderin' your doxie so close to Xmas an' not bein'—"

"It was Sunday the 21st last time I knew," said Jake. "Hildy stayed home and I . . . flew somewhere. Where, though?" He rubbed a knobby hand across his forehead. "That's it, yeah. That's why I'm so fuzzy." He glared at the robot. "Somebody used a brainwipe on me."

Leaving the stunrod resting across his coppery lap, Shux spread his hands wide. "Don't go lookin' at me," he said out of his mouth grid. "We don't use nothin' that rough here at Murderers Home. Like I been tryin' to tell you, Mr. Pace, this here is one of the nicest pre-trial detention stations you could want to be dumped into. Some of 'em is really . . . 'scuse me."

Zzzzzummmmmm!

Jake knuckled his temple. "Pink and white flower," he muttered. "Pink and white flower . . ."

"You goin' to pieces an' babblin', sir? 'Cause I am allowed to administer a—"

"A carnation." Jake snapped, not very effectively, his fingers. "Yeah, it was a carnation in someone's lapel. It started hissing."

"That there ain't standard operatin' procedure for carnations, sir."

"This was an unusual carnation, Shux, old buddy," Jake told him. "Used to deliver a mindwipe to be in gas form. It effectively erased away yesterday."

"Could be that there's all for the best. That way you won't never be haunted by the memory of the brutal and disgustin' crime you committed, allegedly committed."

Jake asked, "Who did I allegedly kill?"

"A Miss Palsy Hatchbacker." Shux's round eye holes widened. "Mind if I ask you somethin' sorta personal, Mr. Pace? In your more intimate moments with a mistress name of Palsy Hatchbacker, what did you call her? I meant to say, both her front and her hind names ain't much in the way of bein' romantic. So how the—"

"Never even heard of Palsy Hatchbacker." Jake, slowly and cautiously, stood. This time the dizziness lasted only a few seconds. "That's who they say I murdered, huh?"

"With good reason, way I hear tell." Shux was rocking slowly to and fro. "Mean to say, they done found you in bed with the poor girl. You was still holdin' the lazgun an' she, poor wanton creature, was dead as a dornick."

"Where?"

"In bed," repeated the robot. "Big fancy one, as it was described in the initial Federal Police Agency report. All ornate an' made out of real brass with little frilly—"

"I mean, in what sector of this great land of ours?"

"Chi-2. You recollect whereat that is? It's the Upper Class city built down under old Chicago. At least, when you stooped to folly, you done it in a posh location."

Jake started to pace. "I don't remember Chi-2 either," he said. "Nope, and neither Palsy Hatchbacker nor a brass bed."

"She was a soprano," said Shux helpfully.

"Palsy was?"

Nodding his ball of a head, the robot replied, "That's how come she was in Chi-2 at all anyways."

"To sing?"

"That's whereat they caught you, Mr. Pace, at the Chi-2 Underground Operadrome. Did you know what the cheapest seat for that particular concert was goin' for? $306. Imagine shellin' out three hundred an' six smackers just to hear the Girl Commandos sing patriotic songs an' do empty-headed skits pertainin' to—"

"I thought you told me they found me in bed."

"In one of the corridors under the stage they got a bunch of property rooms," explained the robot guard. "You was in the one designated Prop Room 24C. That's whereat they keep all the prop beds. Got somethin' like seventy-four of 'em stored in 24C."

"Then I could hardly have helped being in bed." Jake halted, leaned against his cell wall.

Shux chuckled. " 'Spose not, now you mention it."

"What exactly was I doing when Bullet Benton grabbed me?"

"Sleepin', with a most contented smirk on your puss."

"And he stungunned me before I even woke up?"

"That there's standard operatin' procedure for dealin' with crazed sex killers."

"Standard for Benton in dealing with anybody." Jake folded his arms. "The Girl Commandoes I've heard of. They've been touring the country with this patriotic review of theirs, raising money for the Veterans of the Brazil Wars Relief Fund."

"You ought to have heard tell of 'em, seein' as how you was havin' a torrid affair with their lead soprano."

"Nope, I didn't know her at all. I've got no idea why I—"

"Well, I do, you helpless dupe!"

Jake pivoted. "Hildy!"

A slender and lovely auburn-haired woman had materialized on the platform next to the toilet. She was dressed in a two-piece suit of shimmering neosilk and Jake could see parts of the grey cell wall through the slightly out of focus projection of her body.

"This isn't much of a cell they've stuck you in."

"You ought to see where I'd be if Bullet Benton hadn't put in a good word."

"That bastard," observed Hildy, tossing her hair. "I had to hustle three Supreme Court lawbots out of bed to get the papers needed to force him to tell me where you were. That's why it took so damn long to arrange this tri-op call to—"

"Excuse me, Mrs. Pace, ma'am," put in Shux as he left his rocker. "Would you like me to close the toilet seat before you an' your spouse continue talkin'? See, we're goin' through a sort of transition, fixin' up the cells an' all the work ain't quite—"

"Who's he?" asked Jake's wife.

"Something between my guard and my nurse," Jake answered. "What about springing me from this joint?"

"We're working on it, Pilgrim and I."

"Who?"

"John J. Pilgrim; he's an attorney."

"What about Odd Jobs, Inc.'s regular attorneys?"

Hildy frowned. "Most reputable attorneys won't touch your case," she informed him. "Since John J. Pilgrim works with Lost Cause, and they have to touch some of the—"

"Lost Cause? That's who's going to try to get me out from behind prison bars?"

"We don't have bars here," said Shux. "Not since the last—"

"He often speaks metaphorically," said Hildy.

"Oh, that's okay then. I ain't programed to appreciate that fancy stuff."

"Pilgrim's a damn good lawyer, Jake, and I hear he's pretty much got his drinking under control," said Hildy. "And with me outside gathering evidence, we'll have you out of this dump by Xmas."

"Fat chance," laughed Shux. "Oh, dang! 'Scuse me for buttin' in, Mrs. P."

Jake was easing closer to the tri-op platform. He could hear the faint sizzling his wife's image made, even above the frequent burbling of the toilet. "Listen, Hildy, somebody slipped me a brainwipe."

"Seems too subtle for Bullet Benton to have done, doesn't it? A clout on the skonce is more his style. Any idea who else might have done it?"

"None whatever."

"Then you can't remember yesterday at all?"

"Not a single . . ." He hesitated.

"Jake, what is it?"

" '. . . they're our favorite floaties . . .' " he all at once sang. "What the devil is that from?"

"Jingle for a breakfast food commercial. Why?"

Wrinkles formed across his tan forehead. Finally he answered, "Don't know exactly. When you asked me if I remembered anything from my last twenty-four hours or so, that fragment of jingle popped into my head."

"Anything else?"

"I left our place in the skycar, I woke up in this famous bastille. In between, nothing," he said to the image of his lovely wife. "Why was I in Chi-2?"

"The girl who pixphoned said she had important information."

"About what?"

"The Big Bang Murders."

Jake took a step backward. "Somebody named Palsy Hatchbacker was going to tell me something new about a case that's been stumping government agents and police officers all over the world for weeks?"

"So she promised," replied Hildy. "Myself, I thought it was a scam. But you insisted on whizzing out there in one of our skycars. When you saw her in that seethru plaz Girl Commando uniform, there was no diverting you, Jake. Then, too, she mentioned they might let you sit in on piano when they did their Tribute To Jazz medley midway in—"

"Forget my alleged vanity for the nonce," her husband urged. "Consider this instead. The girl was knocked off. The logical conclusion is she knew something."

Hildy asked, "Did she pass on any information to you before she was murdered?"

He shrugged forlornly. "At the moment I don't know."

"What's in your head can be got out. A few sessions with a skilled braindredge medic and his crew can fish out what you did yesterday, every darn bit of it. Why did you pick that room full of beds, by the way?"

"Maybe because it sounded more comfortable than one full of swords and pistols. You don't think I had any—"

"No, I trust you."

"Well, I'll be doggone." Shux was located once again in his rocker, stunrod across his knees. "That there's either love or stupidity, an' mighty impressive either way."

"Your robot is sweet," remarked Hildy. "Okay, now, Jake, the next thing we have to arrange is—"

"I can't wait for a gang of medics to go through all it takes to give me back my last day," he told her. "We'll have to use Skullpopper Smith."

"That psi in Cleveland Ruins?" Hildy shook her head, auburn hair swirling. "He's loony, Jake. When he uses that quirky skill of his to untangle knots in people's brains, the results can be dangerous or even—"

"Nonetheless, Skullpopper can do the job in a couple hours," reminded Jake. "Pixphone him and set up an appointment for six tonight."

" 'Scuse me, sir," put in Shux. "But you can only have projected visits from your kin an' your lawyer. It don't sound like this here Mr. Smith is neither."

Ignoring him, Jake said to Hildy, "When Secretary of Security Strump pixed from DC last week he hinted he'd like Odd Jobs, Inc. to take a crack at the Big Bang thing."

"Fairly broad hint. He openly offered us $500,000."

"Damn it," said Jake slowly. "That's a hell of a low

fee for fiddling with something that's stumped every government intelligence agency."

"Not only stumped," said Hildy. "It's caused the demise of six agents. Three of them from Strump's own Internal/External Security Office."

Jake turned his back on his lovely wife's image, locked his hands behind his rump. "The job is worth a million bucks, at least."

"Didn't know there was so much money to be made in detective work," said the robot.

"We specialize in difficult and unusual cases," Hildy said to Shux. "Cases normal agencies won't go near, cases even our government has given up on. We have a knack for that sort of thing."

"Okay, we'll do it for $500,000." Jake faced the projection platform. "Pix Strump and tell him."

"How exactly are you going to investigate anything while incarcerated in Omaha?" inquired his wife.

"That's part of the deal with the Secretary of Security," Jake said. "Strump gets us for the bargain price of $500,000 *only* if he gets me clear of here by no later than noon today, Omaha Heartland Time."

Hildy smiled. "He just might be able to swing it."

"Of course he will," Jake assured her.

CHAPTER 2

———◦◦►———

Jake ducked into the cabin of the maroon skycar, frowning. "Two sixteen in the afternoon you get me out," he remarked as he settled into the driveseat.

"There was even more red tape than I'd anticipated." Hildy, clad in a one-piece neosilk flysuit, was fastening her safety gear.

"Such as?"

"Well, for one thing Secretary Strump tried to drop the price down to $250,000 because—"

"That tight-fisted bastard. Why?"

"Because as an alleged sex killer you won't be as effective at investigating as—"

"Who says sex killers don't make good detectives? The whole proud tradition of private investigation rests—"

"Strump also thinks you and I won't be as good a team henceforth, because I'm going to be peeved about your being in bed with that zoftig blonde who—"

"Was she?" He punched out a flypattern on the sleek sewdoleather dash.

"Which?"

"Blonde. I don't remember anything about her."

"Not even why she was in bed with you wearing nothing save a dinky pair of lace-trimmed plaz glopanties?"

16

While their skycar rose silently up through the bleak, grey afternoon, Jake thought. "Nope," he said. "Funny, but I don't even remember what she looked like when she pixed us."

"Not *us* but you. Palsy Hatchbacker insisted on speaking exclusively to you, Jake."

He shook his head. "When we get to Cleveland I can have Skullpopper—"

"Is that where we're heading?"

"Since it's long past two and my appointment's at six, we—"

"It isn't, though. Skullpopper can't take you until tomorrow morning at ten," explained Hildy. "Personally I think you ought to turn yourself over to a legit braindredger who—"

"Read my release papers again, love," he said, punching out a new pattern on the controls. "I have *one* week to clear myself. Then its back to this corn-belt bedlam. Why the hell can't he see me tonight? Did you offer him a double fee?"

"Triple. But he's tied up completely with a Banx executive who can't remember where he put his hand." Hildy gazed down at the snow-spattered agridomes they were zooming over.

"Guy wants to know whether he's been dipping into the till or patting the wrong vice-president's wife's behind?"

"Nope, he's a cyborg and the main vault in his Banx branch opens only to his ten fingerprints. With the hand missing he can't—"

"Speaking of money. You did, didn't you, finally convince Strump to pay us the whole $500,000?"

Hildy said, "More or less. The important thing was to get you out of that awful mechanized hoosegow before they did you serious—"

"More or less?"

"Now don't bellow and bounce, okay? I know when we formed Odd Jobs, Inc. some years back, we vowed never to compromise on fees. But . . ." She reached over, touched his hand. "I wanted you free fast."

"Okay, I understand." His smile was only partially bleak. "What are we getting?"

"$250,000 in cash," Hildy told him, "and that's in front. It's already in our Banx account, I checked before teleporting out here to the Heartland."

"And the rest in what? They're not still trying to unload those Nixon half dollars or those Great American Men of Letters Harlan Ellison two-bit stamps that came out with the glue tasting like sour chicken noodle soup? You didn't tell him they could pay us in—"

"Actually, Jake, we might even make more this way," his beautiful wife said. "Remember last year when the presidents had a brainstorm about raising money so not so many old folks would have to go live in Social Security Reservations? The—"

"That's another thing that is so nifty about working for the United States Government these days," he said. "What other country has a pair of Siamese twins for President? Ike and Mike Zaboly. There are two names worthy of being enshrined with George Washington, Abraham Lincoln, Thomas—"

"I'd list them on the same rung with Harry Truman, Warren Harding and Ronald Reagan," she said, folding her arms beneath her breasts. "Besides, it isn't sporting to make fun of the handicapped."

"Handicapped? Mike and Ike Zaboly are barely Siamese twins at all," Jake asserted. "Attached at the elbow. Their staying together is simply an affectation."

"I understand they only have one funny bone between them and so an operation might—"

"Aha!" he exclaimed. "I see what's coming."

"You gave me your word you wouldn't bellow and scream when—"

"It *is* Flago!"

After a few tense seconds Hildy admitted, "Well, yes."

"You let those identical oafs pay us off in Flago national lottery tickets."

"They have an awful lot of them left over, Jake, since the initial public response hasn't been as—"

"I'll tell you what my initial response is. Ike and Mike Zaboly, along with Secretary of Security Strump and his entire staff can stuff those Flago ducats up—"

"That'll take you one heck of a long time, since there are 250,000 of the damn things."

"Holy moses, Hildy. Hasn't any of my savvy rubbed off on you?" he said, bouncing on his skycar seat. "When we do work for the government, any government, we get cash money. No stamps or bonds or lottery tickets or free passes on the space shuttle or—"

"Well, screw you, Jake Pace." She was angry. "Next time you commit a brutal sex crime I'll let you rot."

"Rot? Rotting I could handle," he said. "But when you are convicted of a sex crime in this part of the country they rehabilitate you. Rehabilitation in the Heartland means being taken out of the sexual competition permanently. Not only that, they also fix you so you don't even *think* about ladies or gents or whatever the opposite sex may be for you. They even fix your brain so you start having doubts about the theory of evolution."

Hildy patted his hand. "I wouldn't want you not to be able to think about Darwin once in a while," she said. "You have so little fun in life as it is. If it weren't for going to bed with blonde sopranos behind my back every so often you'd—"

"Ho! I see it all now. You really believe what that Piltdown Man of the Federal Police Agency believes. You think I—"

"The Piltdown Man wasn't a true primitive, he was a fake."

"So's Bullet Benton. The point is, Hildy, you truly believe I did fool around with that unfortunate girl."

"You were in bed with her, Jake. Bullet showed me pictures of the whole shabby scene and I—"

"What pictures?"

"Police vidcam footage. That was the second or third time I pixed the bastard, after one of our Odd Jobs, Inc. stringers in Chi-2 called to alert me to the fact you'd been . . . been discovered in a compromising position."

Jake asked, "Did you copy 'em?"

"Of course, sure." Hildy leaned, pushed a button on her side of the dash.

A small panel slid aside, revealing a tray-size viewscreen.

"Bullet only showed me about sixty seconds of what they got." She touched a crimson button.

There on the screen was Jake, naked, spreadeagled on a brass bed. He did have something of a smirk on his face. Sprawled next to him was a dead girl. Blonde, in her middle twenties, the fringed bed cover touching her only from the knees down.

"Jesus," said Jake, grimacing.

Hildy touched another button. The picture froze, the girl's naked body came closer. "Kilgun used at close range."

"How long had she been dead when they found us?"

"Roughly an hour."

"How'd the FPA know where to look?" He was hunching forward, studying the dead girl's face.

"Palsy Hatchbacker was supposed to go to dinner with some of the Girl Commandos after the final show," said his wife. "An Xmas party for the top singers in the bunch. When she didn't show, a couple of them came back to search for her. They're the ones who found you two down in the prop room and screamed for the Feds."

"And Bullet Benton just happened to be in Chicago?"

"I'm looking into that."

"Let me see the full picture again, but keep it frozen."

She complied. "You don't remember any of this?"

"Not a damn ... there it is!" He tapped the screen, grinning.

On a patch of yellow floor between two of the prop beds, a fourposter and a double bunk, lay a crumpled flower.

"Does that mean something?" Hildy arranged for a closeup of the pink and white flower.

Jake scratched at his temple. "That's a real carnation, not made of plaz," he said. "But a hole's been drilled through its center. Yep, the mindwipe gas was sprayed on me through that blossom."

"Who was wearing it at the time?"

His thoughtful frown deepened. "It's a smaller carnation than you usually see on lapels."

"Looks to be a Chiisai carnation, a genetic mutant developed in Tokyo-3 at the turn of the century. Some ladies wear them in their hair, others use 'em to decorate their—"

"Nope, I'm near certain it was worn on a lapel. Who would wear such a dinky flower?"

"A dinky person."

"A midget . . ." Jake shook his head, exasperated. "Damn, I get a fleeting memory of a diminutive little guy, but I can't hold onto the picture."

"Really a midget?"

"Yeah. No. Not exactly."

Hildy asked, "Want to see the whole tape again?"

"Later on, when we get home to Connecticut," he said. "Did you bring a copy of the Hatchbacker girl's call?"

"Sure." She depressed two more buttons.

The dead girl was alive again, smiling fetchingly out at them. She was wearing a seethru plaz tunic of military cut. ". . . I absolutely have to talk to *Mister* Pace," she was saying. "It's not that I don't absolutely trust and respect you, Mrs. Pace, but . . ." Palsy hesitated, glanced back over her shoulder.

"Hold it," said Jake. "She's in her dressing room, isn't she?"

"Yes, the top Girl Commandos get private dressing rooms with pixphone alcoves."

"Somebody opened the door in her dressing room while she was asking you for me."

Hildy brought a blowup of the narrowly open door to the dash screen. "Bit fuzzy and lacking in definition."

"Funny place for a foot." His forefinger ticked at the screen. "See it? Dangling there about . . . what? . . . three feet from the floor."

After fiddling with buttons and dials, Hildy said, "Best I can do, Jake. All we can see is that brown shoe and a tiny bit of checkered trouser leg. Small shoe, could be somebody was holding your midget up."

"Yep, doubt it's a babe in arms. Fellow with a foot

that little might go in for dwarf carnations," he muttered. "It could be . . ." He snapped his fingers.

Hildy smiled hopefully. "You've remembered something else?"

"Nope," he admitted. "Thought maybe some enthusiastic finger-snapping would job my noggin."

"At least we know someone was listening in on Palsy's call."

"Two someones. The little gent and whoever was toting him."

"Shall I roll the rest of this?"

Jake shook his head. "Let's save it until we're home," he decided, leaning back. "Right now you better pix Secretary Strump and suggest he rush teleport us everything he's got on the Big Bang killings."

"Already did that," she said. "Stuff'll be waiting at home."

Jake watched her pretty profile for a moment. "Damned if you aren't nearly as efficient as I am." He leaned, kissed her.

"At the very least," she agreed a few seconds later, giving him an affectionate punch in the ribs.

CHAPTER 3

———•—•———

Let's, before we proceed any farther, fill ourselves in on what the Big Bang Murders are. You probably heard something about them via SatNews or on your vidwall. Could be you even read about them in your homeslot faxpaper, unless you live in a sector where the printed and faxed word is overseen by the Nonviolent Majority.

At any rate, the first death occurred six weeks and a day ago in the newest South American country, Brasil-Dos. On a calm, sultry November afternoon Generalissimo Francisco Feminino blew up. Along with him went his nearly new palace, his entire staff, his second wife as well as his latest mistress and all the foliage and wild life that had covered a collar of land exactly twenty feet wide all around the palace. When the Policia Segreda's demolition experts let out the news that they could find absolutely no trace of what it was that had caused the despot to explode, DC assumed the bomb experts were simply too inept to sift the debris properly.

Five days later, however, Sir Fergus O'Breen, Prime Minister of Free Ireland, as well as his stately home in Downpatrick and a goodly batch of his associates and relations, were blown to smithereens. The following Tuesday General Mjomba Bata Mzinga, a strongman ruler of Black Africa—22, exploded along with his landcar and bodyguards, while en route to the opening festivities of the Kool Nobac Cigarets International Boogie Woogie Festival. By the second week in December five internationally prominent business tycoons, including Otto Zeppelin, inventor of the fantastically popular digital cuckoo clock, had also exploded, taking their mansions, chalets, wives, lovers and trusted staff members with them into oblivion.

In not one of these cases has a single investigator, not even crackerjack agents from five of the United States' top intelligence and espionage agencies, been able to find even a trace of a clue as to what is causing the explosions. The assassin, or group of assassins, seem able to destroy the intended targets completely without harming anything beyond the environs of the target area. Considerable unease has spread through the civilized world, fear has touched both throne rooms and boardrooms. The media, in places where it is not curtailed or controlled, has long since taken to calling these inexplicable deeds the Big Bang Murders.

Over fifteen agents worldwide, and that figure includes several top men from various United States agencies, have met their deaths while investigating the Big Bang assassinations. Interestingly enough, none of the agents was killed by an explosion.

CHAPTER 4

———•—•—•———

Raucous honkytonk piano, slightly off key, came clattering across the twilight grounds of their secured estate in the Redding Ridge Sector.

"Is my sound system on the fritz?" Jake popped out of the freshly landed skycar and started jogging across the docking strip toward their sprawling glaz and neowood home. A gentle snow was flickering down, dabbing at the plaz dome that sheltered the landing area.

"Hold on," suggested his wife as she caught up with him and tugged at his sleeve. "It's probably only Pilgrim."

Jake slowed, left eye narrowing. "That drunken shyster broke through our security setup and is whomping on my antique upright?"

"I gave him a temporary electrokey," explained Hildy. "At the time I wasn't certain I could get you clear of the pokey, so—"

"He's got a lousy left hand." Jake used his own electrokey to open the ground level door. "Sounds like a landtruck trying to molest an elephant."

"For a lawyer, he's not all that bad," she remarked, following her husband up the ramp to the living room area.

"Oh, I ain't the gene splicer or the gene splicer's son," a wine-blurred voice was singing loudly just

26

above them. "But I can get into your jeans before the gene splicer comes!"

Jake reached their living room first. Hands on narrow hips, he stood on the threshold scowling.

A small red-haired man of forty-eight, his perspiring face rich with bright splotchy freckles, was energetically attacking the keyboard of Jake's white upright piano. Tilted at a rakish angle on his shaggy head was a derby borrowed from Jake's large collection of vintage headgear. "Oh, I ain't the microbiologist or the microbiologist's son," bawled John J. Pilgrim. "But I can slip you a nice little thing till the microbiologist comes." Playing with only his right hand for a few bars, the speckled attorney fished a plaz bottle of wine out of a pocket of his rumpled green blazer.

"Unk." Jake shuddered. "I never thought I'd see anyone guzzling Chateau Discount Wine under my roof."

"Oh, I ain't the cosmonaut or the cosmonaut's son ... have you considered pleading insanity, Pace?"

"Hildy's the one for a plea like that. Hiring you is ample proof of total goofiness and—"

"Actually," said the sozzled little lawyer, "I don't think they'll ever bring you to trial. Too bad in a way, because I'm at my best in a courtroom setting."

"I thought barrooms were more—"

"Listen here, Pace, how'd you like a sock in the kisser?" Pilgrim jumped up off the piano bench, stepped on a discarded bowler hat and fell flat on his face upon the buff thermocarpet.

"You nitwit, you nearly crushed my authenticated Fats Waller derby." Jake sprinted across the wide room, ignored the sprawled attorney and scooped up the caved-in hat.

"Fear not," said Pilgrim as he erected himself, in

swaying stages, up from the floor. "I happen to be wearing the Waller."

"No, you dimwit, that's the authenticated Willie The Lion Smith hat. Didn't you look at the nameplates when you swiped—"

"Swipe is a nasty word, Pace. Don't go slandering my good name or—"

"Your name's about as good as—"

"Fellas," cautioned Hildy, stepping gracefully between them. "We're all on the same side, remember?"

Jake snorted. "What side is that?"

"Well, we all fight for truth and justice along—"

"I'm also a champion of the underdog." Pilgrim took a gurgling sip of his wine.

"Chateau Discount Muscatel With Dr. Pepper Added?" Jake had read the gaudy label, then turned his back on his wife and the weaving Pilgrim.

"The muscatel with Dr. Brown's Cola added has a somewhat more delicate bouquet," said John J. Pilgrim. "Yet for my sensitive palate this particular vintage is—"

"Have you learned anything?" inquired Hildy. She got hold of the attorney's arm, guided him over to a glaz slingchair.

"I've learned that nothing can substitute for a mother's love." He toppled into the chair, legs sliding wide. "I've learned that nothing can touch the heart like the innocent laughter of a child. I've learned—"

"She means about the case," cut in Jake.

"Oh, that." Frisking himself, the rumpled lawyer located another bottle of wine. "This might be more to your taste, Pace. Sparkling Burgandy With Hawaiian Punch & The Minimum Daily Requirements of Vitamins A, B—"

"Jake's case," reminded Hildly.

". . . And sometimes Y and W," muttered Pilgrim.

He sampled the newfound wine, smacked his lips appreciatively and set the bottle down on the carpet. "You have considerable pull in DC, Pace."

"Enough to get me out for a week."

"Those dippy peas-in-a-pod who call themselves the Presidents of the USA dote on you," continued Pilgrim. "They know you and the missus will venture where angels and FPA agents fear to tread. Therefore, they won't allow you to be processed as a convicted sex killer." He leaned back, smiling, hands steepled.

His chair tipped over, spilling him on the floor.

Hildy gathered him up, got him arranged in the chair again. "We can't count on a pardon for Jake," she said to Pilgrim. "No, we're going to have to solve Palsy Hatchbacker's murder and turn the real killer over to the Feds."

Pilgrim laughed. "That'd make Bullet Benton, excuse the expression, dump in his diapers for sure," he said. "Problem is, you're going to have to solve the Big Bang Murders as well. Doing all that in a week is a hell of a task."

Jake said, "You work with Lost Cause, so you've tangled with Bullet Benton before. Any idea why he was in Chi-2 when the Hatchbacker girl got killed?"

"He wasn't," replied Pilgrim. "He was skiing in the Arabian Alps."

"He's the one who arrested Jake," Hildy pointed out, "and used that damn stungun on him."

"Anonymous tip," said the redheaded attorney. "Benton got a pixcall, scooted to the teleport depot and arrived in Chi-2 in plenty of time to catch Pace with his britches, not to mention his tunic, sox and skivvies, down."

Jake sat on the edge of the piano bench. "Any details on that anonymous tip?"

"Public-minded citizen doing his or her duty, reporting a disgusting crime," said Pilgrim. "This particular public-minded citizen used a very expensive voicemuffler, meaning there is absolutely no way to get a usable voice print."

Hildy asked, "Where was the call made from?"

"It was a blankscreen pixphone call, made from the Chi-2 operadrome." He leaned, swooped up the wine bottle to take another long guzzle.

"Might've been the little guy with the carnation," mused Jake, stroking his chin.

Gathering up his collection of wine, Pilgrim wobbled to his feet. "I've got to pop out to the Dakotas to see an Amerind client," he announced. "The regional cops claim he's the Wounded Knee Strangler."

Hildy got a grip on his arm. "We appreciate your efforts, John J.," she said. "I don't know if there's anything further you can—"

"I'll keep my eyes and ears open," the freckled little lawyer promised, nearly falling over a floating end table. "I prefer hopeless ones, but even a near hopeless case like this stimulates me. You can always get a message through to me via Lost Cause."

When Hildy returned from seeing Pilgrim out, she made a disapproving face at her husband. "You didn't even wish him good-bye."

"Maybe I should've launched him with a bottle of Chateau Discount champagne." He shifted on the bench so he faced the keys. "I didn't really think my cause was lost until he swam into view."

Hildy seated herself in a floating chair, crossed her long handsome legs. "Someone knew you were going to visit Palsy Hatchbacker," she said. "Looks like that somebody may've also tipped the Feds."

"Same somebody also knocked off the girl." Jake,

hunched slightly, began noodling out a slow blues on the piano.

"Do you want me to come along when you visit Skullpopper Smith?"

"Nope," he said. "While I'm recapturing my memories of the fateful day, you better skim through all the information Secretary Strump turned over to us."

"We already know quite a lot about these Big Bang doings."

"But nowhere near enough," her husband said. "Nobody, for instance, seems to know what the motive is. See if you can spot one."

"You don't think this is purely political?"

"Do you?"

Hildy poked her tongue into her cheek. "No, I have a hunch this transcends politics," she said finally. "Especially since nobody's jumped up to claim credit for all the explosions, and nobody's made any demands, outrageous or otherwise."

"The killer isn't a terrorist either," he said. "Not in the traditional sense."

"Who is he then?"

Jake grinned a thin grin. "Ask me again in a week."

CHAPTER 5

———————◆———————

The dazzling pimp flashed open his neofur greatcoat with both beringed hands to reveal his badge. "Feast your peepers on that, daddy," he invited Jake, smiling grandly with gold-plated teeth.

The badge was made of platinum, studded with rubies, and it identified its wearer as a member of the Ohio Urban Police.

"Very fetching," said Jake, who was leaning his left buttock against the border barrier that was barring his entry to Cleveland's Ghetto Village area. "Goes nicely with your earrings."

The cop touched one of the bangles decorating his black earlobe. "It's a bit gaudy, ain't it?" he said. "I tell you, you understand, I ain't truly a pimp or a panderer. But if you is going to police Ghetto Village, you got to deck out accordingly. Lots of very rich folks reside herein and they insist on accurate detail."

"I have an appointment with one of them." Jake produced his ID packet from an inner pocket of his two-piece cazsuit.

"You ought to've seen me when I was patrolling over in Gay Life City," said the disguised police officer, motioning for Jake to pass his IDs across the hip-high barrier. "Pace, Jacob. Age 34." He looked up, squinting, from the packet. "Them eyes don't look slate grey. . . . They is more volcanic ash grey if you ask me."

"The robot who filled that in had a very poor color sense."

"I might even go so far as to dub them orbs *mean grey*. Special when I contemplate how you is glaring at me this very minute . . . Odd Jobs, Inc." He slapped his fur-clad side with the collection of identification cards and plates. "So you is that Jake Pace." He ran the entire packet through a scannerbox in the barrier post.

"Yep, mean-eyed Jake Pace of Odd Jobs, Inc. Can I come in now?"

"No bells rung when I ran your stuff through, so you is okay." He tossed the packet back, then fished a floppy rod out of an inner coat pocket. "Got to check you for weapons now, daddy."

Pung!

"Stungun," explained Jake as the nozzle end of the rod made a noise about his armpit.

"Yeah, that's right. Stungun goes *pung*, kilgun goes *glump*, gasser makes a *bloob* noise to warn us." He flipped a toggle that caused the barrier to swing silently aside. "Didn't I see you on the SatNews last night? You was mutilating a convent girl or something."

"That was probably another Jake Pace." He stepped from spotless plaz paving onto cracked and buckled asphalt.

"No sir, man, it were you." The cop nodded to himself. "Said you was a sex killer."

"Alleged sex killer."

"Well, the box already say you can come in, so I ain't going to argue," he said, tapping the scanner with the fat ruby in his pinky ring. "But try not to go pulling any new sex kills hereabouts, you hear."

"It's a deal."

"See, you got to be a pretty well to do mother 'fore you can afford to dwell here in Ghetto Village," he explained. "What you see before you is all the color and excitement of Black and Hispanic urban ghetto life of half a century ago, but with none of the hazards. Take them hookers yonder, for example."

Leaning in a doorway of a seemingly burnt-out tenement a half block away were two black girls in short crimson skirts and tight lime-green sweaters. They both beamed invitingly when the cop gestured in their direction.

"They're actually androids," said Jake.

"Exactly, daddy. So if you was to get yourself a little of what in bygone days they called jelly roll offen either of them, you could rest assured you wasn't going to pick up the clap, the gunk or the glop. 'Cause you can't nohow get no disease off an andy. Further, you ain't going to get rolled, knifed or disemboweled. Why not? Because any of that would be a violation of the basic rules of robotics. Like I been saying, you understand, when you live here you get the thrills of ghetto life with none of the handicaps."

"Live here yourself?"

The cop laughed, gold teeth glittering in the thin winter morning sunlight. "Me? I wouldn't live here even if I could afford it. I got me a condo in the Youngstown Sector, all glaz and plaz. Let these rich mothers try to recapture they roots and they history."

Nodding, Jake moved on. It was about six minutes shy of ten. All around him rose very convincing redbrick tenement houses, nearly half appearing burned out and falling into ruin. A quite believable black derelict was relieving himself at the mouth of a shadowy alley, a paper-bagged bottle of wine tucked under one skinny arm. Jake could see enough of the label to tell it was a Chateau Discount wine. Farther up the block he passed a narrow restaurant whose dying neon sign advertised Texas Chili. There were two pool halls next, then a ramshackle hotel. In front of the hotel, the Ebony Plaza it was called, three gang-jacketed black youths were stomping a sidewalk Santa Claus. From the third floor of an apartment a woman's voice screamed for help, the sound rising above the noise of dozens of loud, fuzzy radios.

". . . sin an' a shame, yes, brothers and sisters, it's a sin an' a shame the way you livin'! God don't like it!" A street preacher was stationed in the gutter, shaking his fist at the loiterers in front of the corner liquor store. "God don't like your lowdown ways! He don't like your sinful livin'! He don't. . . ."

Jake continued on his way.

When he first set foot on Skullpopper Smith's block, he didn't immediately sense anything wrong. Up on the rooftop of a grey stone tenement across the street an eleven-year-old Spanish girl was apparently being sexually attacked by seven thickset youths whose neoleather jackets proclaimed their membership in the same gang that was kicking Santa Claus. Another drunk was relieving himself in an alley. At the nearest corner a sidewalk vendor was selling a soft drink to a blind man and overcharging him. All of it was quite authentic and believable.

Jake didn't even turn when he heard rusty wheels squeaking behind him. Just another foodcart being pushed along the rutted street.

Jake rubbed at his nose, slowed.

"How'd you like some ribs, brother?"

A large, wide black man was shoving a battered wagon labeled *Mr. Ribbs*. He was out in the street, some six or seven feet from Jake.

"Sounds good," Jake said, grinning in a rather grim way. "Nothing like nice greasy spareribs, thick with fat, to perk up one's morning. I'll just tug out my wallet and we'll make us a deal."

"And, oh my, you is going to love this deal," promised the white-coated vendor as he dipped a big hand into the bowels of his cart.

Jake's hand emerged from his tunic first. He held not a wallet but a stungun.

Zzzzzzunmmmmm!

"What you think. . . ." The vendor jerked back, stiffening. His hand came out of the hole in the cart. He was clutching at a silvery kilgun. After making a few faint gurglings, he collapsed into the gutter.

"Androids don't use aftershave," Jake said to the stunned man. He glanced in all directions, started for the unconscious man.

Zzzzzzizzzzzle!

It came from the corner, from the kilrifle the soda man was wielding.

Jake threw himself flat, went rolling back swiftly across the sidewalk. When he smacked into a porch step, he flipped himself up into a tenement doorway.

Zizzzizzzzle!

The second blast of the kilrifle missed him, too. It hit, however, the outcold Mr. Ribbs salesman and his body began to shake and shimmer. In less than a minute there was nothing but gritty dust inside his white suit.

Sirens were hooting, alarm bells commenced clanging.

"Get your ass in here, Jake!" suggested an annoyed voice from above.

Jake glanced up at the opening doorway at the top of the steps. "I'm a few minutes early for our appointment, Skullpopper."

"Just look at the kind of lowlife you attract into this lovely neighborhood," said Skullpopper Smith. "I'm paying a fantastic mortgage payment each and every month so I can dwell in peace and security. Then you come dragging all your rowdy friends into Ghetto Village."

"You mean all this isn't part of the effort to recreate your ethnic past?" He climbed the steps, quickly.

"There ain't no wildass sidewalk assassins in my past," Smith assured him. "Now get on inside before any more folks get slaughtered."

CHAPTER 6

———•—◆—•———

The robot whistled. "Zowie!" he exclaimed, steam hissing appreciatively out of his hearslots. "What a smasheroo pair of gams!"

"Why, thank you, Bozo," said Hildy sweetly as she slid the rest of the way out of the idling landcar.

"Oops," said the tin-plated parking attendant, clapping a metal hand to his mouthole and clicking off the tiny jets of steam. "Didn't realize it was you, Mrs. Pace."

Smoothing her short spunplaz skirt, Hildy said, "Think nothing of it."

"Most of the middle-aged Westport Sector bimbos who come here like a little flattery and crapola," the robot told her as he arranged himself on the driveseat. "So they got me rigged to spout gross compliments. Even if a broad's got legs like the pillars in front of a neoclassical bank and knees like a bulldog's jowls, I got to ogle and smirk. Sometimes I even clap my mitts like a seal in heat. Remember what a seal was? Furry things with flippers that the Japs killed off up in—"

"Yes, Bozo, I have many fond memories of seals. Right now, I have to see Ross."

"Okay, kiddo." The robot pressed the shift button on the dash. "You really do, by the way, have terrific stems."

"Yes, I know." Hildy went striding across the pink-tinted clients parking/landing lot.

Bozo roared her car two hundred pink yards into a very tight parking slot.

Hildy's low-heel walkshoes made determined clicks on the plaz ramp which went arching out over the sluggish Saugatuck River to the cream-color doors of Wall Street Wally's.

A huge lightsign above the portals made a small barking sound. Its numbers jogged ahead and it now read *Over 7,600,000 Sold*.

"Impressive," murmured the auburn-haired Hildy, stepping through the doorway that had silently opened for her.

The receptionist giggled when Hildy asked for Ross. She was an enormous fat girl, wearing a zebra-stripe sarong. "Oh, heavens, excuse me," she said, blushing from tip to toe. "Whatever must you think of me, Miss. . . ."

"Mrs. Pace."

"Whatever must you think of me, Mrs. Pace?" sighed the immense young receptionist. "I'm new here at the Wall Street Wally's branch, you see, and I still can't get used to the fact my boss has a silly name like Ross Turd III."

"It's a fine old New England name."

"Oh, I know. He keeps telling me Boston has been full of Turds for generations, but that just makes me. . . ." She let out a whoop of laughter, rested her head on her green glaz desk for a few seconds while she quivered with amusement. "Forgive me, Mrs. Pace. Goodness. I'll buzz him."

"Thank you." Hildy turned to gaze out the viewall. Several sooty gulls were swooping at the surface of the river.

"Mr. tee hee hee . . . Oh, golly, excuse me, Mr . . .

tee hee hee hee . . . Um. Mr. Turd, sir, Mrs. Pace hee hee hee is here to see you."

"Send her right in, Blimpie."

"Really, I do wish you wouldn't call me that, Mr . . . tee hee hee . . . oh, the hell with it. Go right on in, Mrs. P."

Ross Turd III was an incredibly handsome and sun-burned man of exactly thirty-five. He had wavy golden hair, sparkling sky-blue eyes and was five feet four inches high. "That pinhead," he said, standing up behind his silver boomerang desk. "I wish to hell I could fire her."

Hildy sat in a platinum-tinted shapehug chair, crossing her long legs. "Can't you?"

"The last time I dumped a fat girl I had Fat Power pickets all over my ramps for weeks. And all seventy-six Wall Street Wally stock and bond shops across the nation were boycotted by the Overweight Liberation Army and the House Committee on Fairplay for Gross and Disgusting People threatened to hold hearings." He shook his handsome head forlornly.

"I suppose you've thought about changing your name?"

"What?" He'd been about to sit down, but now he bounced up to his full height. "I'm susprised, surprised and stunned, surprised and stunned and dumbfounded, Hildy, that you of all people could suggest such a thing. After all, you're a keen and astute student of American history—"

"I know, Ross, the Turds played an important part in the epic of American—"

"Important and significant, important and significant and unique," he said, sitting, tentatively, down again. "There were Turds on the Mayflower, Hildy. A Turd with Washington at Valley Forge. And who can forget Remington's immortal painting of the Battle of San Juan Hill? There's a Turd in that one, too."

"Even so, Ross—"

"Ah, but enough of my family pride," said Ross Turd III. "What can I do for you, Hildy? Is Jake contemplating further invest—"

"This has to do with a case Jake and I are involved in." She leaned forward. "I'm hoping you can provide me with some information. If I go after it in the usual way, it'll take too darn long."

"I can't betray confidences, even for you." He was watching her gently swinging right leg.

"You know Jake's been accused of murder."

"Yes, but I'm too discreet to mention it to you."

"The information I need has nothing to do with business secrets," she assured the broker.

"I am a great admirer of yours," he acknowledged, still watching her leg. "And of Jake's as well. Ah, well, then, what the devil. Certainly, I'll help if I can, Hildy."

She smiled, relaxing some in her snug chair. "I've been going over, with the new computer system Jake designed, all the data sent to us by Secretary Strump."

Turd sank some in his chair. "Don't tell me anything too secret."

"I already told you, when I pixphoned, that we've been retained to investigate the Big Bang Murders."

"Yes, and I think it's splendid, splendid and courageous, of our government to attempt to rehabilitate Jake in this—"

"For cripe's sake, Ross, he didn't *really* kill that poor dippy girl."

"Of course. All his friends and admirers, friends and admirers and well-wishers . . . but get on to how I can help you two swell people."

Hildy said, "The government intelligence agencies, ours and those of most other nations, have concentrated on the assassinations that are, seemingly, of a political nature."

"And they've missed something about the explosion murders that've occurred in the private sector?"

"Right you are," she said, smiling across at him. "When you compare all the Big Bang deaths, certain patterns, heretofore ignored, pop up. The most intriguing thing is that every single murder, private and public, helped the status of certain stocks." She dipped slender fingers into a slitpocket in her scant skirt. "I've brought a printout of them."

Ross Turd III was frowning. "Surely, Hildy dear, you're not hinting that someone would be so crass as to commit murder, commit a series of brutal murders, simply to influence the stock market?"

"Not hinting, Ross, stating," Hildy informed him as she unfolded her list. "The company whose position has benefited most is an outfit called Newoyl. They're based out West and before I—"

"Newoyl has been climbing," he agreed. "The death of Mjomba Bata Mzinga makes Black Africa—22 look much more iffy as a new source of oil, and the blowing up last week of Sheikh Moumic Moutaab also dealt a blow to the cause of real oil. He was the key man in the Federation of Oil Billionaires."

"Okay, I looked into who the major shareholders in Newoyl are," Hildy continued. "It proved to be trickier than I had anticipated. Turns out, after you sort through the fake names and dummy holding companies, that 52 percent of Newoyl is owned by something called Novem, Ltd." She rested her list on one pretty knee. "This Novem outfit also owns impressive hunks of every other company that's taken a great leap forward because of the Big Bang killings."

He nodded, saying nothing.

"Even using the sophisticated, and sort of unorthodox, equipment Jake's designed I can't find out a darn thing about Novem, Ltd. Not even an address or a pixphone number that's legit."

The handsome stockbroker cleared his throat.

"Well?" asked Hildy.

"This is what you came to me to find out about?"

Her head bobbed up and down. "It is, yes," she said. "Now, though, I get the feeling you're too scared to tell me."

"Scared isn't the accurate word," he said. "Apprehensive, apprehensive and cautious—"

"Apprehensive and cautious and chickenshit." She rose. Walked to his desk. Placed her fists on the desk top, glaring down at him. "C'mon, Ross, this is important."

He held up both hands, as though he were afraid she'd come leaping across the desk to pop him one. She had, he well knew, done such things to people. "I honestly don't know who runs Novem," he said. "I do know, however, they're becoming increasingly powerful and secretive. Powerful and secretive and nasty."

"How nasty?"

Turd III rubbed his fingers across his cheek a few times. "Well, people who try to dig too deeply into the true structure of Novem sometimes have accidents; actually they frequently have accidents."

"Fatal accidents?"

"In some cases," he quietly replied.

Hildy moved back in the direction of her chair. "Looks like I'll have to keep digging."

"You could. . . ."

She spun, eyeing him. "Could what?"

"Talk to the Reverend Gully Lomax."

"That sanctimonious fascist? Reverend Gully Lomax, Chairman of the Board of the PlainKlothes Klan."

"Him, yes. You have to admit, Hildy, they're an improvement on the Ku Klux Klan."

"They dress better," she conceded. "But what does the rev have to do with Novem? His name didn't show up on any of the—"

"I happen to know, though I wouldn't like to be credited as the source of this information," said Turd carefully, "that Reverend Lomax has been trying to buy up Newoyl stock. He hasn't had much luck."

"He might know more than you do about the competition, about Novem."

"Exactly, yes, Hildy." Standing, he brushed his hands togther as if he'd just touched something dirty. "Since you can teleport to the national PKK headquarters in Houston in half a jiffy, you might just be able to get some info quickly. That is, if Lomax will talk to you."

"He'll talk to me," Hildy said.

CHAPTER 7

—————•◆•—————

"Okay, okay, we can skip the incense," said Skull-popper Smith, shaking the smoldering contents of the copper saucer into his living room dispozhole.

Jake sneezed twice again. "If you're sure it won't hinder you."

"The incense is merely just for show," explained the lean, middle-sized black man. He wore a tight two-piece white cazsuit decorated with embroidered moons, stars and comets. A scarlet, gold-tasseled fez perched on his luxuriant hair. "So is this getup I wear."

Nodding, Jake asked, "Why does it say Sons of the Desert on your hat?"

"Because I'm a member of the Laurel and Hardy fan club, schmuck. You ought to know that."

"I'm a Wheeler and Woolsey man myself."

"I'm surprised, by the way, to learn you have an allergy. I always figured you as invulnerable."

"Every hero has a tragic flaw." Jake wiped his nose on a plyochief and settled onto the seethru glaz sofa filled with fast-swimming tropical fish.

"Sneezing isn't a tragic flaw." Skullpopper sat, crosslegged, on the bare yellow floor near the head of the sofa. "Hildy told me this was a serious emergency."

"Obviously, or we wouldn't have paid double."

45

Skullpopper smiled. "The $10,000 was snug in my Banx account by 11 P.M. last night. Much obliged," he said. "You might be surprised at some of the rich ladies I number among my clients. Try to stiff me."

"What sort of work do you do for that sort of client?" He stretched out on the couch.

"Get a lot of first love searches." Skullpopper pulled on purple gloves. "These old squacks screw themselves silly till they're fifty or so, then they inevitably get sentimental. Want to remember the first lad they ever slipped between the sheets with. By that time, though, what with years of booze and pills and brainstim, they're too adled even to remember who they boffed last Tuesday let alone thirty forty years back."

"Must give you a glow of satisfaction."

"Five thousand per recall doesn't exactly give me stomach cramps." He placed a gloved-hand on Jake's forehead. "Been getting a lot of ex-CIA and NSO boys of late, too. This new brainwipe system the government is using on retiring spies, assassins and agents has all kinds of side effects. One international spy not only forgot all the top secrets he knew but also how to tie his shoes. I used my incredible psi powers to unravel his brain."

"I want to remember the night of Sunday, December 21 and the hours following."

"Know what kind of wipe was used on you?"

"Something in a gas form."

"Those can be buggers."

"I'm aware of that."

"Want to wager before we get going?"

"About what?"

"Whether you knocked off that dame or not. $5000 says you didn't."

"I didn't, so there's no bet."

Shrugging, Skullpopper said, "I'm going to put you under now. Want to go back and recall your first Xmas first? You in rompers, being carried down in your daddy's loving arms to see the plaz tree. I get quite a few of that sort of requests this time of—"

"The tree was real, it was my mother who did the carrying and, no thanks." The hand felt hot and incredibly heavy on his head.

"What you do now, Jake, is doze off," said Skullpopper. "I got the power to put you in a trance. Falling asleep won't be so bad, but once I get in there and use my gift to clear out the effects of the mindwipe, it's going to hurt. Even though you're out like a light, you'll feel it. "Some quacks promise painless brainprobing, but that's a lot of guff."

"Guff . . ." echoed Jake as he drifted down into fuzzy darkness.

He was aware of nothing for long black seconds. Then lightning began to flash and sizzle, thunder rumbled. His body seemed to be burning, turning to ashes. His skeleton remained, every single damned bone in it throbbing with pain. He wanted to scream, let some of the pain out. His mouth was locked shut.

Jake kicked, flapped his elbows hard against his sides. The pain was going to kill him, rip his brain right out of his skull. If it went on for one more . . .

. . . audience was seeing an immense undulating American flag. But from Jake's vantage point backstage he saw instead a forest of legs and buttocks.

The Girl Commandos, ninety-nine strong, were winding up a medley of war songs that ranged from "Praise the Lord and Pass the Ammunition" to "God Bless Our Nuclear Superiority." Each of the lovely girls, decked out in a star-spangled sarong, held up an electroglo placard that formed a portion of Old

Glory. All except the choirmaster, a hefty redhead, who was circling the vast plazwalled operadrome on an impressive mockup skyrocket.

"That's Miss Hatchbacker in the second row," whispered the aged doorman, pointing out onto the vast stage, "blonde lassy holding a star with her left yonker about ready to flop all out of her skimpy attire."

Jake spotted the girl he'd flown to Chicago to talk to. "Thanks, Mr. . . ."

"Just call me Pop. Fact is, you got to. That's in my Doorman's Guild contract."

"Okay, Pop."

"I wasn't always a doorman."

"A star once?"

"Nope, but I was the *Phantom of the Opera.*"

"Oh, so?" Palsy Hatchbacker had noticed him and nodded, giving him a furtive sideways wink. He grinned one of his less intimidating grins.

"Wasn't in Paris, though," Pop went on. "This was in the Newcastle, Pennsylvania, Opera House. They got the idea they might drum up some interest in their tacky productions if word got around the dump was haunted. It was fun for awhile, then it grew boring. You ever try lurking for eight ten hours a day?"

"My best time's an hour."

"After that gig petered out I moved along to—"

"You still handing out that boring flapdoodle about your tedious, useless life, Pop?" inquired a squeaky little voice.

Without turning, Pop nudged Jake. "Listen to this now, if you want to witness some good-natured kidding." He chuckled. "Better watch what you say, you termite motel."

"I'm not scared of you. You look like the poster boy for terminal cancer."

"Hush up, or I'll turn you into a smorgasbord for woodpeckers."

"Who's this deadpan with you?"

Jake had long since turned to scan the owner of the piping voice. The voice seemed to be coming out of an ugly little wooden man with frightwig yellow hair, freckles that looked like splashes of blood and a glittering red and white checked suit with a dwarf carnation fastened to the lapel. He was dangling, arms and legs spread wide, from the arm of a handsome dark-haired girl in a dark grey one-piece worksuit.

"I'm Jake Pace," Jake said.

"Are you bragging or complaining?"

"Woodrow, shame on you," said the dark girl. "I don't know what gets into you."

"Half the time, sister, you don't even know who gets into you. Wow, you were so drunk last night when you picked up that skyjockey I thought—"

"Really, Woodrow, that's no way to talk to a lady."

The dummy spun his head completely around three times. "Where? Where is she? I didn't hear her come in."

Smiling, the female ventriloquist said, "My name is—"

"Trina Twain," Jake supplied. "I've seen your act."

"What was a nice guy like you doing in toilets like the ones we usually play?" Woodrow wanted to know. "Until we got this job I thought a urinal was a required part of niteclub decor. Once in Bridge-port—"

"Be quiet for a minute, Woody."

"If I ever shut up, bimbo, you're finished. You ain't going to get by on looks," her dummy told her. "And as for your figure, I've seen better builds on flag-poles."

Pop tapped Jake's arm. "Number's coming to its big climax."

"That's where Bobbi up on the firecracker drops her undies and we see she's got the words and music to 'The Star-Spangled Banner' inscribed on her fanny," exclaimed Woodrow, rolling his tiny pink eyes at Jake and leering. "And with her backside there's room left over for the six most popular Xmas carols of the season."

"Woody, do be still. You'll have to excuse him, Mr. Pace," said Trina, smiling.

"You're a damn good ventriloquist," he said. "Now if your material matched your—"

"Ventriloquist? This bimbo can't even toss her voice across those horsey teeth of hers," Woodrow piped. "I do all my own talking."

Up above the audience of five hundred the mock rocket was exploding, splashing thousands of red, white and blue sparks across the dark dome of the high ceiling. Bobbi came parachuting down, waving a replica of the original thirteen colonies flag.

A moment later, amid much enthusiastic applause, the Girl Commandos came marching off the stage single file.

Palsy caught Jake's arm as she went by and tugged him along with her. "I have a half hour before I have to meet some friends for dinner," she said. "I wish you hadn't been standing out in the open. Come along, down this ramp."

"When I talked to you this afternoon," he said, following her down a dim-lit ramp which led to an even lower level of the underground theater, "I didn't get the idea there was any danger in my being recognized."

"Oh, I don't know. Maybe there isn't," the blonde-haired young woman said. She reached forward, pushed a swing door open. "I may simply be going bonkers. I don't know."

"You do know something."

"Well, yes, I'm certain of that," she said, hurrying him along a curving corridor. "At least, I think so. Sometimes it all seems possible, but then again I get absolutely certain. In here."

He reached around her, opened a thick door labeled Prop Room 24C. "This is where you want to talk?"

The low-ceilinged room was full of beds, dozen upon dozen of them. Four-posters, camp cots, brass beds, wrought iron beds, hospital cots, hammocks, cradles.

"I'll feel safer here than in my own dressing room." Palsy seated herself on the edge of the quilt-covered brass bed, motioned him down beside her. "Why were you talking to Woodrow and Trina?"

"Mostly Woody was talking to me."

"I don't much like her. No, it isn't exactly that. Trina is okay, but that dummy is such a little prick," she said. "Except she is Woodrow, too."

Jake remembered something. "When you were talking to me on the pixphone this afternoon, someone started to walk into your room. That was Trina, wasn't it?"

"The two of them, yes. That's why I had to get up out of the image pickup area for a minute, to shoo them out," she said. "Of course, it's tough to get much privacy in this troupe at all. Ninety-nine girls plus our band. It's almost as awful as my college dorm was."

Jake asked, "What do you know about the Big Bang killings, Palsy?"

"Maybe something important."

"And you don't want to go to the Federal Police Agency or the National Security Office or—"

"No, that's too risky. I have my career to think about," she answered. "Even seeing you like this may futz up things. Being in a show that's so bloody patriotic means—"

"Okay, so tell me what you know."

"It has to do with when I was in college, Mr. Pace. I graduated in '99."

"Not very long ago."

Palsy insisted, "This isn't just a schoolgirl fantasy. I decided to contact you because I've admired you for some time now. I've read about you in *Time-Life* and *Mammon* and all sorts of other magazines, seen you on TV being interviewed on such shows as Sleepy Joe Bryan's *Blab!* I have the impression you can be trusted."

"I can."

She took a deep breath. "When I was in college I majored in Commercial Nutrition," she began. "That's how I came to know about the process. In fact, there are only a few people who do. I really think it has to be someone—"

"Whoa now," he interrupted. "Tell me about this process. What is it?"

"At first this may sound very silly, Mr. Pace, but . . . please, we're having a private conversation."

Jake shifted on the bed, saw Trina Twain and Woodrow coming toward them.

The dark girl said nothing, even the freckled dummy was silent. Smiling, Trina lowered the dummy. In her now visible right hand she held a lazgun. She aimed it right at Palsy and fired.

A line of white light leaped from the barrel and stabbed into the blonde girl's breast. She grabbed hold of Jake's hand. "They're our favorite floaties . . ." she said in a pale, singsong voice. Her grip tightened for a second, then she died.

Jake shook free of her dead touch, went for the stungun in his shoulder holster.

"Take a nap, sappo," suggested Woodrow.

A plume of misty yellow gas came spitting out of the carnation on the dummy's checkered lapel. It caught Jake in the face, rushed into his mouth and nose.

He took a nap.

CHAPTER 8

————•◦•————

"Why so pale and wan?" Jake asked the image of his wife on the dash phonescreen of his parked skycar.

Hildy had short-cropped sand-brown hair, her usually tan face was a stark, indoor white, she wore a high-collar two-piece charcoal-grey bizsuit and a severe pair of decspecs. "Tell you momentarily, but first fill me in on your search for your lost day. Was it painful?"

"Somewhat, yeah," he admitted. His vehicle was sitting in a secured park/land lot just outside Ghetto Village. The neon signs of the exclusive suburb throbbed and blinked in the early afternoon. "Worth it, though."

"Do you know who killed her?"

He nodded, saying, "I saw the deed done. A lady ventriloquist name of Trina Twain did the actual shooting. I don't as yet know who's behind her."

"Could she have been acting on her own?"

"Nope, this is a conspiracy for sure," Jake assured her. "Are you flying someplace right now?"

"To Houston," his wife answered. "Hence the clever disguise. But finish your story first."

"One of the classic ingredients of a conspiracy is a cast of more than one," he resumed. "So far there are

. . . were, rather, three. Trina and two black chaps who tried to kill me on Skullpopper's doorstep."

"Jake," she said, making a small gasping sound, "are you okay?"

"I'm in mint condition, but one of my assailants was transmuted to ashes when his buddy's kilgun blast hit him instead of me."

She shuddered. "They might have been sweeping you up, sending you home to me in an urn."

"What I'm curious about, Hildy, is how anyone knew I was going to visit Skullpopper."

"Secretary Strump knew," she said, a frown on her newly pale face. "Yes, I mentioned it to him when I was setting up the deal to get you out of the pokey. Do you think he's got a leak in—"

"Has to," said Jake. "I double checked our home security system last night after that discount wino went staggering off. No bugs or taps. And I just went over my skycar."

"What did the Hatchbacker girl tell you?"

"Nowhere near enough. Trina and her dummy . . . that's who was wearing the carnation that mindgassed me, by the way, her snide little dummy."

"I assumed as much when you mentioned there was a ventriloquist in the woodpile. That little foot we saw on the phone tape belonged to him, too."

"Little putz named Woodrow," said Jake. "He and Trina snuck into Prop Room 24C before Palsy could even get to the point."

"Didn't she tell you anything?"

"About her college life mostly. And as she was dying she sang that cereal jingle. The one for Bloaties, the Ballooned-Oats Breakfast."

"A dying message?"

He hunched one shoulder. "Not sure yet."

"Where'd she go to college?"

"I'll be checking that."

"I suppose this Trina Twain is no longer touring with the Girl Commandos."

"Nope, she gave notice and vanished while I was languishing in Murderers Home," answered Jake. "Turns out she wasn't a regular, just a last-minute replacement for the lady juggler who usually did the warm-up act. Been with the tour less than a week, only since the juggler got clumsy and fell off a pedramp in the Northfield Sector of Minn-2 and broke both legs."

Hildy said, "So somebody planted Trina and Woodrow to watch Palsy."

"Appears so," he said. "What did you get at the Wall Street Wally's outlet?"

"A lot of admiration from the parking 'bot," Hildy said. "Ross, after I expertly cajoled him, gave me a possible source of information on Novem, Ltd."

"He doesn't know who they are?"

"He doesn't, and he broadly hinted I'd be better off letting my inquiry drop."

"What's the lead?"

"The Reverend Gully Lomax."

"That button-down racist bastard? What in blazes does he have to do with—"

"Seems he would like to own a bigger hunk of several of the companies, most especially Newoyl, that Novem is into. Ross suspects Reverend Lomax may know something about his chief rivals."

"Who are you?"

"I'm Suzie Miller, roving correspondent for *Pure, the Racist Weekly*," Hildy informed her husband. "En route to the PlainKlothes Klan's Houston offices to interview Lomax. I hinted that we at *Pure* were seriously considering him for our Bigot of the Year award."

"He bought that?"

Hildy lowered her decorative spectacles and fluttered her long eyelashes at him. "I might go so far as to say he gobbled it up," she replied with a smile. "I'm seeing him at six."

"Okay, but be careful, huh? He's a nasty fellow, surrounded by a gang of crazed bully boys."

"I'll con him out of whatever he knows, don't fear," his wife promised. "Where are you bound?"

"Not sure. Maybe to Palsy's old alma mater, once I find out where it is."

"You be careful, too, Jake. Don't let 'em turn you to dust."

"Not just yet. Love."

"Same to you." The screen went blank.

Jake leaned back in his seat for a moment. He hadn't mentioned the fact to Hildy, but the session with Skullpopper had left him a little shaky and unsettled. "Once more into the breach," he urged himself, sitting up and pushing out another number on the skycar phone.

Secretary Strump himself answered. He was a stocky, pugnacious man, one year away from retirement. When he recognized Jake, he whapped his realwood desk with a large freckled fist. "Have you seen these?"

"Hold them up."

"These filthy sheets." The Secretary of Security held up a gossip faxoid.

"Quit quivering with rage," suggested Jake, "so I can read the headlines."

"I can tell you, Jacob, neither Mike nor Ike is at all pleased."

"*The Kind of People You Molest Reveals Your Personality*, that can't be the headline that's annoying the presidents. *Lose 23 Pounds A Week On The Dis-*

count Wine Diet! Is that it? I noticed Ike Zaboly was getting a little thick around the—"

"This one!" Secretary Strump abandoned one of the scandal tabloids so he could poke a front page headline on the other. "*Government Throws Away Your Tax Dollars On Killer PI!* Both the presidents are—"

"That's me? The killer private eye?"

"And as if what *The National Intruder* has to say isn't awful enough, look at *Muck.*" He displayed the second weekly. "*Sex Killer Blows Your Tax Bux!*" He was flipping through the pages. "And feast your eyes on the article they ran. I look like I have three chins and warts."

"Sue them. You can prove you don't have warts, can't you?"

"Oh, certainly. That would look marvelous. My trying to establish that I'm not . . . what is it they dubbed me . . . 'a senile tax squanderer who, when he isn't stuffing Your Tax Dollars into the sleazy pockets of criminal private cops, adores dressing up in female garb to molest crippled children.' Both the presidents, Jacob, are in a tizzy."

"How'd the *Intruder* and *Muck* get their information?"

"What information? I don't have so much as one dress or gown in my entire—"

"The news that you hired Odd Jobs, Inc."

Strump lowered the scandal sheet, blinking. "I hadn't considered that," he said, taken aback. "Did you issue a press release?"

After grinning bleakly, Jake said, "Hildy and I don't believe in that kind of publicity. Somebody in your office leaked."

"Hardly possible. Each man and woman in my organization has undergone the most rigid—"

"It's not only *Muck* who's being told what my wife and I are up to," cut in Jake. "I was anticipated on my visit to Cleveland this morning."

"What? What?" The thickset secretary rose halfway out of his realwood swivel. "Are you suggesting—"

"I'm suggesting that two louts posing as ethnic androids tried to kill me about three hours ago."

"How can you be certain this particular attempt on your life has anything to do with the Big Bang case?"

Jake laughed. "I've got a hunch."

Absently balling up *Muck*, the Secretary of Security said, "I can run another check of my people, but—"

"Do that," agreed Jake. "Meanwhile, I don't plan to report to you too often or too openly."

"Come now, Jacob, we're paying you $500,000 to investigate—"

"I don't, no matter what you hypnotized Hildy into accepting, consider lottery tickets legal tender of coin of the realm," Jake told him. "But since you did get me out of that pesthole I—"

"Those Flago tickets could net you a bloody fortune. Not to mention such additional prizes as a trip to the Poconos, a silverplated—"

"I'll be signing off now. Start weeding." Jake shut off the call.

After another minute or two of leaning back, eyes shut this time, he sat up and tapped out a new number.

The small pixphone screen remained black, but a voice said, "Oho! It's America's favorite killer. How're you, Jake? How's your skinny wife?"

"We're both doing as well as can be expected," he said. "I want some quick background information, Steranko."

"Then why not use that vaunted new computer system you installed at the old homestead?" The screen commenced clearing.

"I have to admit that, at the moment, you're better than I am at digging out the kind of dirt I'm looking for."

"At *any* moment, sweetheart," corrected Steranko the Siphoner. He was a small man of thirty, absolutely bald and wearing a spotless two-piece lemon-yellow cazsuit with matching ankleboots. He was lounging in a lime-green canvas chair in the midst of an impressive electronic clutter. "Since you're an old pal, Jake, and since your toke is in a sling and since its nearly Xmas and my tender heart is even more tender than usual, I'll do what you want for a mere $2500."

Jake grinned. "Very touching, only 40 percent above list price."

The Siphoner said, "There is no list price for this kind of work, cookie." He gestured at the modified computer terminals, wordproz machines, databoxes and not quite identifiable info retrieval devices that surrounded him. "There's a simple reason I'll always be superior to you when it comes to the gathering of data from hither and yon. Scruples."

"Meaning you have none and I do."

"Precisely, old buddy," said the bald man. "I am absolutely shameless when it comes to gathering information. I can, and will, tap any source on Earth or orbiting it. I'll unblushingly listen in as a virginal thirteen-year-old lass goes to confession, take advantage of a mike concealed in the toilet seat of the Queen of England, steal facts from blind grandmothers."

Jake glanced at the dash clock. "Your commercials keep getting longer."

"Listen, since I'm strangely fond of you and that skeletal spouse of yours, I'll charge you a flat $2000 before I even hear what the job is. Even though I know you held up my own beloved government for a cool one million b—"

"$250,000 is what we got. However, if you'd like to be paid in Flago tickets I can go as high as—"

"Make it $1750. But cease the sad songs before my little heart breaks," said the yellow-suited data bootlegger.

"A deal, send us a voucher."

"Which address? Connecticut or the bastille?"

Jake said, "I want to find a girl named Trina Twain."

"What category would she fall into?"

"Show business and espionage. She's a ventriloquist and a spy."

Steranko leaned, ran his fingers over the keyboard of the nearest terminal. He stared at the screen for a few seconds, scowled up at Jake, grabbed up a mike that activated a voxterminal. "TWAIN, Trina. Designation 99S."

From a speaker somewhere beneath his chair a slightly Romanian voice said, "Nonesuch."

"C'mon, c'mon," urged the impatient Steranko. "Go around that obvious ID block, dope."

"Nonesuch. Repeat non . . . *bonk!*"

The dapper siphoner hopped up free of his green chair, turned his back to Jake to peek at the speaker. "Who the hell is that bimbo, Jake?"

"You're supposed to be telling me."

"She's important to somebody besides you, old pal." Shaking his hairless head, he sat again, tapping his yellow-clad right knee with the mike. "Somebody got at all the standard ID sources, as well as every damn unorthodox one. If you believe them, no such lady ever drew a breath."

"That's an expensive process, sponging somebody out of existence."

"Could the wench be government?"

"Don't know, but it seems unlikely."

"Yeah, it costs big dough to run a wipeoff like this." He bit his lip. "Tell you what, this is now a challenge to me. Give me a few more hours and I'll track her. No extra charge. When'd you see her last, or have you ever?"

"I did, in Chi-2 on—"

"Scene of the crime?"

"Committer of the crime."

"Check back at sundown if you can. Anything else?"

"As long as I have you on retainer, you might as well do a simple trace for me. Girl's name is Palsy Hatchbacker. I'm—"

"The unfortunate victim."

"The same. I'm interested first off in her college years."

Making a small grunting noise, Steranko kicked at a databox that was within kicking distance. "Did you get that name, dodo?"

"Got her, boss," replied the gunmetal box.

"Looks to me, Jake, as though some gang with one hell of a budget is out to . . . hold it."

An orange light atop the waist-high box had started to blink.

"Go ahead," instructed Steranko.

"HATCHBACKER, Martha 'Palsy,'" spoke the box. "Majored in Commercial Nutrition. Attended Poorman's Harvard in Boston Sector, 1996-1999. Studied extensively with Professor Dickens Barrel, by the bye."

"So what?" said Steranko.

"He's missing."

"So he is." The Siphoner snapped his fingers. "Want something on Prof. Barrel, Jake?"

"He was doing food and nutrition research at Poorman's Harvard, wasn't he?"

"Right, much of his work financed by the food industry," said Steranko. "Especially by Foodopoly, our largest food conglomerate."

"Professor Barrel vanished about a year ago, didn't he?"

"Without a trace."

Jake was rubbing his fingertips along his cheekbone. "Foodopoly manufactures Bloaties."

"Along with untold other types of edible garbage," said Steranko. "Want me to dig you up stuff on the prof or on the Thrasher family who control Foodopoly or—"

"Nope, you concentrate on unearthing Trina Twain," Jake told him. "I'll get back to you."

"Where you off to?"

"Boston," Jake answered.

CHAPTER 9

There was Bullet Benton.

The massive blond Federal Police Agency cop was looming at the other end of the tree-lined hallway, his muscled arms full of infospools, file folders, toktapes, voxboxes and several bulging nosee plyosax.

Jake sat down on a green bench, crossed his legs and leaned back, waiting.

Bullet stomped toward him, chortling. "Returning to the scene of the crime, huh?" he boomed out.

Glancing around this corridor of the underground campus of Poorman's Harvard, Pace said, "What crime?"

"Isn't this where you first seduced that poor kid, while she was still a virginal coed?"

Several of the infospools and folders had *Dept. of Commercial Nutrition/Highly Confidential* stenciled on them in glored. "I have a permit slip from the Dean of Nutrition to look at that stuff," Jake said.

"What stuff, Jake?" Bullet plopped down next to him, causing the bench to rattle.

"Background material on Palsy Hatchbacker and on the researches of Prof. Dickens Barrel."

The federal cop deposited his armload on the grassy floor. "Let's see the permit."

Pace produced a rectangle of yellow fax paper.

Bullet took it from him. He tore it in half, then in

quarters, then in eighths. Tossing the pieces away, he said, "You don't have it now."

Jake grinned. "Why are you interested in what she did in college?"

"Grist for the mill," replied Bullet. "See, Jake, I'm going to see to it you end up castrated and permanently brainwiped. At the very least. When I get through perusing this, I'll know more about that pure sweet child than even you do."

"I don't know much more than her name."

Bullet laughed and the flowers in the wall vases quivered. "You can claim that now, but when I get through digging—"

"What about Prof. Barrel? Why are you interested in him?"

"Who says I am?"

Jake indicated two folders with his foot. "You're hauling off everything the department has on him and his researches."

"No, I left behind his wedding pictures and some recipes for pineapple upsidedown—"

"Did you work on his case?"

"When he disappeared? Naw, that went to the Missing Persons Squad," answered the FPA man. "And those nurfs can't even find their own families with both hands and a road map."

"Figure Barrel took off voluntarily?"

"Yeah, sure, with that pretty little sloe-eyed coed he was so cozy with." Bullet nodded, strong jaw outthrust. "All these middle-aged smartasses go bonko over underage lovelies sooner or later. Like you just did."

Jake casually picked up the top folder pertaining to the missing professor. "Picture of the lass in question in here?"

"Hey!" Bullet snatched it out of his grasp.

A triop snapshot fluttered free, fell to the grass at their feet.

Jake got it first. It showed a thickset, grey-haired man in a one-piece labsuit. He was smiling, modestly triumphant, and holding up a beaker flask with something greenish and foamy within. There was a young girl in labclothes on either side of him. The one on the professor's right was Palsy Hatchbacker and the one on the left was Trina Twain. Both of them were about five years younger.

Jake put the picture in the hand Bullet had been grabbing for it with. "The one with the dark hair was his sweetheart?"

"She worked with the old goat back then, came back to do grad work," grumbled the cop. "She and the professor dropped from sight last year. You figure it out."

"Didn't know about her connection with him." Jake frowned.

Stuffing the photo safely away, Bullet said, "Did you know they still have the death penalty out in Utah?"

"I did, yes."

"And do they hate sex killers out there," he went on. "I remember when Kevin the Ripper went on trial—"

"Even you can't get me tried in Utah for a crime committed in Illinois, Bullet."

Bullet laughed. "Venue," he said as the bench ceased shaking. "I think I can get a change of venue. Either try you in Utah or, if I'm really extra lucky, Nevada. Now in Nevada, Jake, they don't exactly have a full-time death penalty but they got murder bingo. You take a chance and end up with anything from death in the gas chamber to $400,000 in cash and prizes. Fate decides." He bent, grunting, and gathered up the material he'd beaten Jake to. "If we can wait a few months, it looks like Hawaii is going to vote the DP back. Over there in that tropical paradise they let six guys with machetes go after you. Nice and messy."

"I figure to solve this whole thing by the end of the week," Jake assured him.

"No, you won't, buddy." He rumbled to his feet. "I am going to make sure you get tagged for this one. I owe it to you and the missus. So long now, nice talking to you."

"Always is."

When the large Fed had disappeared around a bend in the grassy corridor, Jake moved his foot.

Hidden under it was something that had fallen from one of the plyosax.

"Some helpful clue," said Jake, when he'd picked up the object and examined it.

What he had in his hand consisted of two circles of gold-tinted plaz held together with a screw. There were numbers on the larger outer circle and letters on the smaller inner one. Emblazoned in gloletters across the center of the smaller circle were the words, *Captain Texas Secret Decoder*.

Jake stood up and dropped the thing in his pocket.

The lightsign over the saloon doors halfway down the corridor flashed *The Beer Joint (R) (C) 2002, 2003 by Foodopoly. One of 7,626 identical dives serving needs of the college youth of America and of the civilized world in general*. It was a fairly large sign.

What attracted Jake to the college hangout, as he was making his way along the underground hallways of Poorman's Harvard toward the AdminPlex, was not the multicolor sign but the raspy singing and offkey piano-thumping that was blaring out.

"Oh, I ain't the teleporter, mama, and I ain't the teleporter's son," piped a smeared voice. "But I can move you, baby, till the teleporter comes."

Jake pushed inside the place, which smelled, thanks to the aircirc system, like stale beer and the latest prohibited drugs.

"Oh, I ain't the soy nutritionist, mama, or the . . . 'Ah! The very personage I am seeking."

John J. Pilgrim, the tipsy attorney, was seated at a glaz piano in the center of the dim-lit saloon. He had a derby tilted at a rakish angle and a beer mug was making foamy rings on the slick glaz top of the upright.

Five beautiful young ladies, dressed in scanty two-piece sophsuits and froshsuits, were gathered around the rumpled little lawyer.

"Don't cease your playing," pleaded one.

Jake went striding through the mostly empty tables. "Is that one of my derbies?"

Pilgrim whipped off the topper, gazed inside. "No, it is apparently the property of a gentleman entitled Crazy Otto."

"It is one of mine." Jake yanked it out of his hand. "Do you know what an authenticated Crazy Otto brought at the last Parke-Bloomingdale auction of Pop-Jazz Memorabilia?"

"$1924," said one of the lovely coeds. "My Cousin Nels bought it. Who are you?"

"It's best you don't know, Marigold," advised Pilgrim. He left the piano bench, intending to stand. Instead he fell over into the believable sawdust. "Don't mix Chateau Discount Burgandy Blended with Diet Pepsi and Storm Trooper Light Ale."

"Wise words." Jake jerked him up off the saloon floor. "Were you looking for me?"

"Got my client off earlier than I expected. Proved he couldn't be the Wounded Knee Strangler because he was actually the Deadwood Peeper. Ironclad alibi. Voyeurism trial a week from Tuesday in the Dakotas Municipal Law Arena."

Jake guided the wobbly little man into a dark corner. "Have you come up with something?"

"Bullet Benton has confiscated all the official background material on the deceased Miss Hatchbacker."

"Yeah, that's what he told me when we had our recent chat."

"You shouldn't talk to any FPA agents, Pace. Let me do the . . . oops!" He tipped over, landing in a sitting position in a booth. "Well, may as well have one more little pitcher of—"

"Do you know anything else?" Jake sat opposite. "Otherwise I'll continue on my way to the administration people and see if—"

"I have something." Pilgrim held up a forefinger, noticed it was smudged and examined it. "Imagine that, the black rubs off the piano keys. Inferior modern craftmanship. I doubt the immortal Crazy Otto ever had to—"

"What do you have? Besides a sooty finger?"

"Wait, be patient." He was searching himself and arraying the contents of his saggy pockets on the tabletop. "There's the murder weapon from a famous murder case and—"

"That's a beer opener."

"If it were just a beer opener, Pace, it wouldn't be labeled Exhibit B. Also have a pair of lace pants with the day of the week embroidered on them in what an expert witness swore is Serbo-Croatian. Piece of toffee with cat dander stuck all over it. Piece of lint. It's odd to find lint in a sincloth suit, unless they're putting it in to fool the . . . Ah, here we are." He pushed a crumpled slip of paper across.

Written on it in a scrawly hand was: *See LS-2 Grady Sunbloom. Re: Palsy. Obsessive Infatuation.* "What's this mean? Does this Sunbloom know Palsy?"

"No."

"Then why—"

"I defended Sunbloom last year for allegedly harassing Princess Lulu of Monaco-3," explained the lawyer. "He suffers from what is technically known as a Worshipping From Afar Compulsion. In the case of the zoftig Princess Lulu he was not, during a spring vacation from Poorman's Harvard, afar enough to suit her."

"What's it got to do with Palsy?"

"She is also on this gent's list," explained Pilgrim. "I only realized that sometime after you heaved me out into the snow at your palatial estate in—"

"What list? This Sunbloom guy keeps a list of the ladies he idolizes from a distance?"

"Exactly. Common symptom in our media-goofy society. I defend one of these poor mutts every three or four months."

"Does he know something about her murder?"

"He knows everything about *her*," replied the little lawyer. "He fell for her when she was an undergrad at this very college. Never spoke to her, but began to collect data on the lass. See? He has more info on her, including bootleg copies of everything the old U has, than Bullet B made off with right under your snoot. Sunbloom's even got—"

"And he's still here at PMH?"

"He's always going to be here." Pilgrim made an exasperated face. "That's what LS-2 means. Lifetime Student, Second Class. He has a scholarship forever."

"I remember now," said Jake. "Before our enlightened US Government dreamed up Flago, they had Schoolo. The top ten prizes were lifetime scholarships to the school of your choice."

"Sunbloom won one of them in '93. He's stuck down here for the rest of his natural life."

"I'd like to talk to him."

"All arranged. I told him that as soon as I located you I'd escort you to his digs." Pilgrim executed a swaying rise from his bench. "Come along, Pace. The game's afoot!"

He took three wobbly steps and fell over.

CHAPTER 10

———————•◦•❖•◦•———————

Hildy was in a glaz booth that floated high above the audience, a thousand strong, in the immense outdoor Texas theater. Down on the stage the Plainklothes Khorus was finishing up a hymn and up here in the control room the producer and the director of the *Hour of Supremacy* were sobbing.

"Whenever they come to them lines about motherless children havin' a hard time," said the chubby blond producer, "it just 'bout tears my heart clean out."

"Me, too," blubbered the director, a lean young man in a white buckskin suit. "And I'm a test-tube baby born of a surrogate mother. No reason for me to be sentimental at all." He dabbed at his tiny little eyes with a polkadot bandanna.

"I had my mom committed to a Home for the Annoyingly Old just a scant month ago," said the snuffling producer. "Couldn't stand the ol' bimbo. But, wowie, when I hear that song it whops me right in the guts."

"Fascinating," murmured Hildy, making a note in the large notebook perched on one handsome knee.

The producer glanced away from the monitors to scowl at her. "I don't want to see nothin' about me snarflin' like a babe in print, lady," he warned.

"Nor I," said the director, pushing back the brim of his white Stetson with his thumb. "We don't want anybody to get the idea we is softies." After blowing his tiny nose on the bandanna, he hid it away in a fringed pocket of his jacket.

Down on the stage the Reverend Gully Lomax was striding out of the wings to join his guests for today's show. He was a large fleshy man of fifty-one, clad in a three-piece white bizsuit and white cape. Glowing on his breast pocket was a scarlet cross and the familiar PKK logo. His silver hair was a nest of gentle waves.

"What's comin' up, brothers an' sisters? What day of days is almost upon us?" he was saying into his silver tokstik. "Oh, an' it's gonna be a glorious day tomorrow! A glorious day that celebrates the birth of a great man, the greatest man in the world, present company excepted. Yessir, it's comin' up on the birthday of Jesus Christ!"

Everyone of his thousand followers sighed, "Amen!"

"Now, what ought we to do? What, Lord, ought we to be thinkin' about? On Christmas Day each an' ever' one of you miserable sinners got to fall down on your worthless knees. That's right. On your knees an' thank the Lord you was born with a *white* skin. 'Oh, Jesus, thanks a million for makin' me white on the outside an' on the inside. Thanks for this white skin. I could do without this wart on my nose an' these little zits on my chin, but all in all, thanks for ever'thin'.' Once you get that out of the way you still got time to examine your soul an' ask, 'What in the dickens am I gonna send to the Revererend Lomax for his Xmas present?' You still got time to get me somethin' by tomorrow, if you ship via UPS-Telepax. I'll be givin' you some broad hints on what sort of stuff to send me in awhile. But right now let's meet our blessed guests on today's Hour of Supremacy!"

"Heartwarming," sighed the producer.

"Give me camera two," said the director. "Pull back, Leon."

There were three guests awaiting the reverend in the mock living room set at the center of the stage.

"Praise the Lord," said Lomax, sitting between a buxom blonde young woman and a gaunt old man of ninety-six. "I got to tell you, Sister Tandem, that the Good Lord surely blessed you plenty when it came to tits. Wow, you got a socko set of 'em!"

"Amen!" said the entire audience.

Tammy T. Tandem glanced down modestly at her impressive breasts. "I thank the Lord for all my gifts, Reverend Gully," she said. She was wearing a seethru plaz two-piece cowgirl suit and a glaz sombrero. A glaz guitar filled with goldfish rested next to her chair. "Ever' time one of my tunes hits the top of the charts, I just get down on' my pretty ol' knees an' give thanks."

"You got a hit what is toppin' the lists right now, ain't you, hon?" asked the reverend as he patted one of her knees.

"I do," she admitted shyly. "According to *Fascist Billboard* and *White Downbeat*, my new vidcaz of 'I Ain't Gonna Marry No Honkytonk Man Nor Any Jigaboo!' is right up there close to the ol' top."

"Praise Jesus."

"Amen."

The old man was ticking in his chair, blinking and frowning. "You're not Gary Nixx," he accused Lomax.

"Nope, I ain't, Mr. LaRue. I am the Reverend

Gully Lomax, founder and director of the Plain-Klothes Klan and host of the highly rated *Hour of Supremacy*," explained the wavy-haired video evangelist. "Now allow me to introduce you to our vast audience. Brothers and sisters, we're honored to have with us a man who dedicated his noble life, up until the time they went an' impeached him in 1991, to servin' this great land of ourn. Let's have a nice hand for Former Vice-President Slick LaRue, ninety-six years young, an here to tell us about his new book that deals with his service to our nation. It's entitled . . . what is the dang title, Mr. LaRue?"

"*How I Screwed America*," answered the ancient Vice-President. "But you aren't Gary Nixx."

"I still ain't, no."

"Then this can't be *Nutrition On The Barricades!*"

"It surely isn't."

The old man slumped in his chair. "My fool public relations firm told me I was scheduled to do Gary Nixx today," he whined. "I've been nibbling on nothing but carrots since dawn. I sat around in your half-wit green room munching on bran flakes before shambling out here."

"Wellsir, the Lord wanted you to be on *our* show today, Mr. VP. An' here you is."

"I loathe carrots. Bran gives me cramps and worse."

"Just lemme intro our final guest of the day." The reverend leaned across Tammy T. Tandem to pat a fat middle-aged man on the knee. "Direct from the Right Sort Of People Only University in Orange Sector, Greater Los Angeles, is Dr. Leon 'Cookie' Cookson. He's gonna tell us about his latest book, which is called *I Oppose Teleportation As A Means Of Enforcing School Integration And While We're At It I Don't Think Much Of The Theory Of Evolution Ei-*

ther. Wow, there's a title that lays it on the line."

"It's catchy," put in Tammy. "You can just about sing it."

"Cookie?" The Vice President scowled. "What sort of name is that for a grown man to have?"

"It's no worse than Slick," sneered the doctor.

"Certainly it is. Slick is manly and devil-may-care. Cookie, on the other hand, is a pantywaist's name," said the old man. "Why, when I was a boy growing to manhood in Minnesota, I had a little runty pup named Cookie. He was a pansy, too."

"At least I didn't boondoggle this country out of seventy-two billion dollars!" shouted Dr. Cookson, rising from his chair.

"It was sixty-five billion and not one penny more!"

"Gents, gents," said Reverend Lomax amiably.

"Give me a close-up of the old bastard," requested the director.

"Whiles we are waitin' for ever'body to settle down some," said Lomax, "lemme get back to tellin' you what I want for Xmas..."

"You giving him the front cover of *Pure*, Miss Miller?" the producer asked Hildy.

"Oh, yes," she responded, smiling and lowering her decspecs the better to flutter her eyelashes at him. "That is, if I ever get my chance to interview him."

"This background stuff, seein' us at work up here, that'll be invaluable," the producer assured her.

"I'd like to see Reverend Lomax's home as well," said Hildy. "I understand it's a transplanted Gothic cathedral."

"Yep, right. Teleported her over from England, from Barsetshire, at great expense. All the funds donated by the reverend's devoted and vast video flock."

"Fascinating," she said. "And this cathedral-home

serves as his headquarters as well? That is all the PKK records and such are stored therein?"

"It's the hot dang hub of the PKK," said the producer.

"Fascinating," said Hildy.

CHAPTER 11

Jake hadn't been intending to visit CalSouth.

This is how it came about.

After interviewing Grady Sunbloom, the eternal
student, Jake had returned to the skycar. The car was
in a parking dome up on Boston Common and as he
went walking toward it a flock of robot carolers came
rolling toward him.

An even dozen of them, three feet high and gilt-
painted, broadcasting seasonal music out of their
voxgrids and flashing their charity slots. *Help The
Brazil Vets!* pleaded the flashsign on the clittering
chest of one. *Rehab Caffeine Addicts!* begged another.
*Junk Food For Africa-26! Glaz Eyes For The Needy!
Doles For Fictioneers!*

"God-rest-ye-merry-gentlemen. . . ."

"Here, here, here," said Jake, stuffing one-dollar
Banx tokens into each of them. "Now, scoot."

". . . let-nothing-you-dismay . . ."

Snow was falling out in the twilight. The flakes hit
the dome high above the lot, hesitated, melted, were
replaced by new ones.

Jake went through the identification and delocking
routine that let him into the Odd Jobs, Inc. skycar.

Settling into the drive seat, he sniffed at the air in
the compartment. A vague frown touched his face.
He shrugged and picked up a tokmike. "Hildy," he

said, "I'm putting this into our system so you can hear it when you're through with the PKK louts."

He cleared his throat away from the mike, and put his seat into a rest position. That session with Skullpopper this morning had left him feeling damned weary.

"Here's part of what Palsy Hatchbacker was, I think, trying to tell me," he dictated. "Dr. Dickens Barrel, financed mostly by grants from Foodopoly, was working on a new and inexpensive way to puff grain for breakfast cereals. He's the guy who came up with the original method for making Bloaties, but that one, involving nuclear power and lasers, is somewhat expensive. What he'd dreamed up, while Palsy and some others I'll get to in a moment were with him, was an incredible new way. One that involved a simple skull implant and the emerging of latent psi powers. Don't chortle. It apparently worked."

Shifting in his seat, Jake gazed up through the one-way seethru roof. He watched the Xmas Eve snow drifting down and speckling the parking dome.

"What Prof. Barrel did was train a group of the PKK undergrads to explode oats into puffed Bloaties. He reasoned that it would be quite economical to implant his gadget and then train workers who'd scored high on latent psi-powers to work in Foodopoly's plants and puff tons of the stuff per day. No nuke power is required, not even much in the way of solar energy." Jake grinned bleakly. "Trouble was, one of his undergrad groups had an accident, that was back in '99, too. One spring afternoon an entire wing of the nutrition lab blew up. Blam! Just like that. Prof. Barrel was unsettled by that and seemed to shelve the whole project. He eventually, early in 2001, worked out a system somewhat less costly than his original one and sold the Foodopoly folks on that. It involves

solar mirrors and no psi. That's how they make Bloaties at the moment. A year ago the professor disappeared clean away. Also vanishing at the time was a
pretty dark-haired young woman named Christina
Parkerhouse. Better known to show business as Trina
Twain."

He paused, yawning.

Since climbing back into the skycar he'd been
feeling increasingly drowsy.

"Hildy, this is what I think, at this stage of things
anyhow," Jake continued. "A—Professor Barrel and
Trina have teamed up and are using his process to
commit the Big Bang murders. If you can blow up a
goodly part of a college campus, you can do the same
for despots and tycoons. B—Trina made off with the
prof and is herself the mastermind. I tend not to believe this one, maybe because I'd hate to accept a ventriloquist as a mastermind. C—The six students who
made up the lab group that had the explosive accident
are the Big Bang gang. Thus far I can not get a list of
their names, but it's likely that Palsy and Trina were
among them. More on that anon. All of this, I have to
admit, I got from a moderately goofy fellow that
drunken sot Pilgrim put me in touch with." He
yawned again, slouching in his seat. "What I'm going
to do, after checking in with Steranko the Siphoner
again, is try to find Trina Twain first off. If I can't,
I'll go for the professor and maybe the student
group."

He let the mike drop into his lap.

There were smells he should have identified earlier.
One was the new plaz smell fresh made skycars always give off, the other was the faint lemony scent of
sleepgas coming out of your entire aircirc system.

"Hildy . . . somebody pulled a switch on me . . .
substituted a perfect replica of . . . damn skycar . . .

like a sap . . . distracted . . . maybe by carolers . . .
walked right in . . . our own secsystem won't allow
gas . . . so they switch . . ."

His chin tilted down, his eyelids fell shut.

A moment passed, then the vehicle started itself and
went rolling toward a takeoff ramp.

Reverend Gully Lomax took off his cape and hung
it over a gargoyle. "No need to be shy, Miss Miller,"
he said to Hildy.

They were alone in the chapel of the refurbished
cathedral, late sunlight was knifing in through the
stained glass windows and making kaleidoscopic patterns on the PKK chief's white dictadesk and the
stonewalled room's six floating glaz chairs.

"Beg pardon?" She arranged herself, crossing her
long tan legs, in the chair nearest to the one he was
settling into.

"About my Xmas present I mean. You can give it
to me now."

Hildy put her left hand to her lips, blushing con-
vincingly. "Hasn't it arrived?"

Reverend Lomax moved to his feet, walked a small
circle and then rested a broad, white-clad buttock on
his white desk top. "Nope, it ain't," he forlornly informed her.

"Are you absolutely certain?"

He nodded his wave-rich head at the white computer terminal resting on the stone floor immediately
below a tongue-out gargoyle. "Not unless it got here
whiles I was on the air just now," he said. "We log
ever' dang one in." He rested his palm on his knee,
leaning in her direction. "Can you give me a hint as to
what it's gonna be?"

"I'd rather it came as a complete surprise."

"How 'bout at least tellin' me how much you paid?

Thataway, Miss Miller, I can better judge how much time I can spare you an' your mag."

Smiling up at him, she answered, "The price is a four-figure one."

He fitted his fingers into the waves of his silvery hair and gazed up at the groined ceiling. "Four?"

"High four."

"I can chat for seventeen minutes with you. Where's your picture takin' feller?"

"He'll be out later in the week."

"What's he plannin' to give me?"

"A digital cuckoo clock."

"Shit, pardon my French, but I got over nine thousand of them buggers down in the crypt already," he said. "He ain't goin' to be allowed to photograph my best side. Not for no cuckoo clock."

"Is the crypt where you store all your business records, too?"

"Is the dang interview startin'?"

"It is."

"Then my answer is, none of your dang business."

"I know you have all the permanent data on the PlainKlothes Klan stored in your own computer system, but I was interested in bulk data, papers, physical mementoes, gifts, things—"

"What a dumb-ass, pardon my French, way to start an interview."

"You're right." Hildy smiled and fluttered her eyelashes. "Suppose you tell me how you came to found the PKK."

"That's more like it," chuckled the Reverend Lomax. "Well now, it were back in the last century. Around the late autumn of 1996 it was when the idea first hit me. I was nothin' more than a local TV evangelist then, out in CalNorth, workin' out of East Oakland. If you know CalNorth, you know they is nostly heathens, atheists and vegetarians thereabouts. Heck, my first Xmas on the air I pulled in less than $900,000 in gifts. I was, take it from me, scufflin'." He lifted his other buttock up onto his wide, white desk. "I'd always been a fan of the old Ku Klux Klan an' I doted on their philosophy. Thing was, Miss Miller, I got to thinkin' that, for all their good ideas, the KKK was no longer thrivin' as it should. Then the answer come to me."

"Go on," urged Hildy, pencil flying over note-paper.

"It was them goddamn sheets," Lomax explained. "You can't make a dignified impression with a bed-sheet over your head. Look back through history. Did Hitler wear a sheet? Did Mussolini? Did Napoleon? Nope. Now, Julius Caesar did, but not up over his noggin with eye holes poked in it. First off I thought of creatin' a uniformed Klan. Give us all snappy paramilitary uniforms with lots of gold trimmin'. But that might've made trouble, since some folks don't like armies."

"A pity."

"Right." He indicated his white suit. "Why not, I asked myself on that fateful day, why not simply go around in civvies? Dress just like ever'body, but give yourself a catchy name. The PlainKlothes Klan. If you're with the PKK, you can go anywheres. You can pass. That's the key. You can be a bigot an' a racist an' nobody can tell the difference. PKK. Best damn idea I ever did have."

"Fascinating." Hildy closed her notebook and reached into her handbag. "Oh, how foolish. Here I have your present right in my purse after all and I forgot all about it."

"You got somethin' worth maybe $9000 in that bitty little thing?" He hopped from his desk.

"Just take a look," she invited.

Lomax rested a beefy hand on the back of her chair and leaned to peek within the open purse she was holding up to him. "I don't exactly see no . . ."

Hizzzzzzzzz!

Invisible mindgas came nozzling up into the PKK leader's face.

Hildy, who was wearing special nostril filters, waited until he'd had a full dose. Smiling, she shut the purse. "Isn't it lovely," she said aloud. Whispering, she added, "Say it's terrific."

"It is terrific," he droned.

"Make your next reply more jovial," she instructed. "Now, go sit behind your desk and tell your security people to turn all the monitors, audio and visual, off in here. Wink, indicating you and I are going to fool around for a spell."

"Yes, miss." He arranged himself back of the desk. Turning toward a gargoyle high up on the wall behind him, Reverend Lomax ordered, "Blank out ever'thin' for an hour, boys. Looks like I got me a hot one."

Hildy asked, "Who controls Newoyl?"

"Novem, Ltd."

"That much I knew before sitting through the *Hour of Supremacy* and your colorful autobiography," she told him. "Who is Novem? Who are the people behind it?"

"I spent near sixteen million bucks tryin' to find out."

"And?"

"Best we got so far is a list of seventy-four folks who may or may not be part of Novem," the mind-controlled reverend replied. "Got data, pictures, even personal effects in some instances. All stored down in the crypt, an' I got a crew of intelligence agents asortin' an asiftin', tryin' to get at the truth. Those Novem buggers are damn tough to run to ground."

"Your crew down below now?"

"Nope, I give 'em the afternoon off 'cause it's Xmas Eve."

Hildy left her chair, circled the big white desk and took him by the arm. "Come along, Gully."

"Where we goin'?"

"Into the crypt," she said.

CHAPTER 12

—•◦—◦•◦—◦•—

Jake woke up.

He was in a room full of smog and the glaz walls all around him were shaking and shuddering. A mighty rumbling sounded beneath him and everything in the big hazy tower, including his teeth, rattled wildly.

"Landsakes, look after the body! Golly whiz!"

Jake decided he was still alive and, therefore, was not the body being talked about. He remained sprawled on the spunglaz Persian carpet, his body bouncing and undulating in time to the hearty earth tremors.

Smog got in his eyes and nose. He sneezed and sat up. "CalSouth," he muttered, recognizing the smell of the foul air.

The earthquake had, obviously, futzed the aircirc system and some of Greater Los Angeles's foul air was seeping in from outside this business tower.

The walls were chattering less, the wide floor was whumping at less frequent intervals.

Jake tried standing and succeeded.

He found himself in a vast meeting room, up some fifty or sixty floors above the late afternoon heat of the Santa Monica Sector of GLA.

A huge licorice-shade plaz oval meeting table floated at the center of the room, surrounded by thirteen lime-green bizchairs. At the head of the table there was, instead of a chair, a glaz coffin mounted on two neowood sawhorses. Inside you could see the portly body of a white-haired man of sixty-four. He wore a conservative two-piece grey bizsuit and his hands were folded across his middle.

Seated nearest the coffin, with one sharp elbow resting on the table, was a lean, dark woman decked out in bright Gypsy garb and laden with massive golden earrings and many bright glittering bracelets.

A handsome, deeply tanned man in a one-piece tennisuit stood near to the slightly swaying coffin, seemingly listening to it with a highly polished stethoscope.

"Golly whiskers, I can't get this darn aircirc to work at all." A pudgy young man of forty was flicking toggles on a wall panel near the far doorway. "Oh, hello, Mr. Pace. Mercy me, forgive us for being at sixes and sevens. These darned quakes play hob with everything."

Pace took a few steps in his direction. "Who might you be?"

"Well, golly, I might be the Chairman of the Board or I might be the Chairwoman," he answered with a boyish smile. "It depends on several variables."

Jake sneezed once again. "Well, who are you as of this afternoon?"

"Bunny's what you call a switchsexual," said the handsome man beside the coffin. "He is always Bunny Thrasher, heir to the entire Foodopoly empire. I'm Dr. Collin Willbarrow, sixth seeded Medical Tennis Player in the West."

"Congratulations," said Jake. "Who kidnapped me and had me teleported westward?"

"Oh, golly willikers." Bunny gave up on trying to clean up the smudgy brown air. "We only want to consult you, my daddy and me."

Jake seated himself at the table. Being knocked out

so much on this case was taking its toll. "That'd be your pop in the glaz box?"

Bunny made his way over to the big table. "He's D.W. Thrasher." He pointed proudly at the contents of the coffin. "One of the great business brains."

"D.W. died seven years ago," said Jake. "How come he's still above the ground?"

"He runs the company." Dr. Willbarrow dropped his instrument into a pocket. "You must've read about it in *Fortune, Barron's* or *BizWeek.*"

"The fact didn't stick," Jake said, shrugging. "Why was I snatched?"

Bunny smacked his lips, annoyed. "We want to hire you. I didn't want to, golly whiz, make you mad or anything."

"So you built a complete simulacrum of my skycar, rigged it to gas me and fly me to some private teleport pad in the Boston area," he said. "Roundabout. Plus expensive."

Bunny spread his hands wide. "Tell daddy that," he said, dipping his boyish head in the direction of the coffin. "Anyway, the point is we want to hire you."

"Hire me for what? I'm already working on a case."

"This may be the same case," Dr. Willbarrow told him, taking a seat at the opposite side of the floating table.

"I already have a client."

"We'll pay you $500,000." Bunny sat, gingerly, next to the old woman in Gypsy clothes. "Golly sakes, I forgot to introduce you to Madame Batota here."

"A pleasure," said Jake.

"For you maybe," she said in a dry ancient voice.

"I don't usually like to play one client against another," Jake explained. "Make the fee $750,000."

"How about $500,000 and all you can eat," countered Bunny.

"Hum?"

"A lifetime supply of Foodopoly products. Start the day with plenty of sinmilk, sewdofruit and Bloaties. For that midmorn snack a steaming cup of NoJava and a packet of Snax, the belligerent little nuggets of—"

"$750,000 in cash money."

Bunny eyed the Gypsy. "Well?"

"Keep your pants on," she advised, gripping the table edge with both bony hands.

She began to shake violently, earrings and other baubles clinking and clattering. A droning hum issued from her mouth and nose.

She jerked upright in her chair, eyes clamping shut.

"$600,000 and that's it," she said in a new voice, deep and masculine with a faint New England twang.

"$750,000," reiterated Jake. "I could sue you all for more than that just on the abduction."

"Bull pucky," said the Gypsy's mouth.

"Oh, golly whizzers, I haven't introduced you yet. Mr. Jake Pace, my late daddy."

"I'll understand if you can't shake hands," said Jake, slouching in his chair. "$750,000."

"I don't believe in too much dickering, sir. We'll accept your charges. Bunny, sit up in your chair and explain to Mr. Pace what he's getting into."

"Yes, sir, daddy." From an inner pocket of his bizsuit he produced a sheet of pinkish faxpaper. "This is a list of private investigators who preceded you on this assignment, Mr. Pace. Ahum. Rex Sackler, Luther McGavock, Ed Jenkins—"

"By the way, Dr. Willbarrow," said the voice of the dead food tycoon, "as long as I have you here. There's a cockroach in my coffin."

"Unlikely, D.W."

"Don't I know when I have a cockroach pitter pattering all over me? Sliding down my snoz, tap-dancing in my belly button—"

"Daddy, please."

"Go on, Bunny."

". . . Race Williams, Max Latin, Cash Wale, Cellini Smith, John Dalmas—"

"I've guessed what all these lads have in common," cut in Jake. "Besides their private-eye careers. They, each and every one, are recently deceased."

"We feel badly about them, Mr. Pace, and—"

"They were well paid," said D.W. Thrasher via the old Gypsy. "Their associates and next of kin are being looked after in a most generous fashion."

"That is true," said Bunny. "Now then, Mr. Pace. About the time the tenth or eleventh private investigator working for us met a mysterious and fatal end, it became darned tough to hire new ones."

"Why not use your own security people?"

Bunny folded his list. "We lost eleven of them before we went outside Foodopoly," he answered. "Since then, as a matter of fact, there have been considerable resignations in the security area. Right now we're down to nothing more than seventy-eight night watchmen named Pop."

Jake grinned. "You hired all those unfortunate colleagues of mine to find Professor Barrel for you?"

"We did," answered Bunny. "The—"

"Anything that SOB developed while working with Foodopoly grant money," said the Gypsy in D.W. Thrasher's voice, "belongs to Foodopoly. I want that psi process of his. He told us it was too dangerous for puffing oats and other grains, but I no longer believe that guff."

"What about the Big Bang murders?"

"Nothing to do with us."

"And the murder of Palsy Hatchbacker?"

"Your problem, my boy," said the food tycoon's voice. "In case they lock you away for that one, we'll expect a refund."

Jake told them, "The $750,000 fee is for my time during the week I have to clear up this whole mess. Anything beyond that goes into overtime."

"Why, of all the outrageous. . . ." The Gypsy opened her eyes. "Excuse it, gents. I got to go to the crapper."

"Daddy was right in the middle of a harangue, Madame Batota."

The Gypsy stood up. "I lost contact with the old fart anyhow," she told Bunny. "Séance is over."

As she went slouching away, Bunny said, "We'll draw up a contract between Foodopoly and Odd Jobs, Inc., Mr. Pace."

"Can you give me any leads?"

"Well, the last two operatives who came to untimely ends," said Bunny, tugging out his list again, "a Mr. Calamity Quade and a gentleman named Doan, were both investigating the activities of a young lady named Honey Chen. It's ironic."

"How?"

Dr. Willbarrow said, "Honey Chen is an actress, one of the hottest things in satvid right now. She stars on a kidopera we sponsor."

"Oh, yeah," said Jake, recalling. "She's on *Captain Texas*."

"She plays the captain's Eurasian mistress," said the doctor.

"The other ironic thing about Honey Chen," said Bunny, "is she was a student of Professor Barrel's."

"I bet," said Jake, sitting up, "she graduated from Poorman's Harvard in '99."

"Golly whiskers, she did," said Bunny, pleased. "You really are a crackerjack investigator, Mr. Pace."

"I am," agreed Jake.

CHAPTER 13

———•◦◦◾◦◦•———

She found him in the kitchen of the restaurant, arguing with six moustached robots.

"You cannot," Jake was insisting to the chrome-plated robot with the biggest chef's hat, "create a perfect chili relleno without a pinch of—"

"But, Señor Pace, my staff and I have programmed into us the culinary knowledge of generations of Chicanos. Recipes which were already venerated when the beloved Father Junipero Serra first set foot on the golden soil of California. *Sí*, and—"

"Nevertheless," Jake persisted, "unless you add that pinch of—"

"Jake," Hildy said quietly. She was herself again, red-haired and wearing a one-piece emerald green skirtsuit.

He noticed his wife, grinned and moved back from the chefbots and the electrostoves. "I was early," he explained to her, "so I wandered out here to have a chat with the boys."

"I figured as much." She took his arm. "You gentlemen will, I know, simply ignore Jake's eccentric notions about Mexican cuisine."

"Eccentric? Who won the Maximillian Ribbon two years back in the Best Guacamole category?" Jake said. "Not one of these gadgets, no. 'Twas me, your gifted spouse who copped all—"

93

"That particular bakeoff," reminded Hildy, "was open only to *turistas*."

"*Verdad*," murmured one of the kitchen robots.

One of the others was eyeing Hildy, sighing, "*Muy bonita*."

"Nix," Jake cautioned him. "Don't ogle."

"He's built that way," said the head chef. "He used to be a gigolo down at a CalSouth—"

"What say we return to our table," Hildy suggested, tugging. "We only have about two and a half hours, going by California Northern Liberal Time, of Xmas Eve left."

"You're absolutely right." He bowed to the cooking staff. "*Adiós*, gents."

"*Vaya con dios*, Señor Pace."

Out in the main dining room of Zorro's Hildy guided Jake through the crowd of diners to a table close to the view window. From up here you could see nearly all of the Frisco Enclave far below. Beyond the lights of the bay city dangled the lights of its bridges, including the recently completed Gay Golden Gate.

"Tell me a little more about your kidnapping," Hildy requested once they were seated.

"Your hair always looks a little frazzled after you've teleported," he said.

"Why, thank you. Now give me some details."

"As I told you on the pixphone, Foodopoly has hired us and they're going to pay $750,000 into the Odd Jobs, Inc. acc—"

"Already have. I checked with our Connecticut computer just before teleporting here from Texas."

Jake said, "Well, the Thrasher clan wants Professor Barrel."

"We want him, too, don't we?"

Frowning, Jake leaned back. "Probably," he said. "He's tied up in this Big Bang business somehow."

"You figure he's adapted his process so you can blow up people instead of oats?"

He nodded. "That's got to be what Palsy wanted to pass on to me, why she blurted out that fragment of Bloaties jingle as she died," he said. "She went to Poorman's Harvard, studied with Barrel. So did Trina Twain, alias Christina Parkerhouse. And so did the next lady I aim to talk with, Honey Chen."

Hildy's nose wrinkled. "That blatant sexpot? She actually studied nutrition?"

"Minored in it, majored in Sensual Dramatics."

"Speaking of old PMH alums," his red-haired wife said, "I'm going to drop in on another one, up in the Portland Redoubt tomorrow morning."

"You got something out of Reverend Lomax?"

"Too much, probably."

"That sanctimonious goon didn't try to fondle you or—"

"Nope, but he did ask me what I was going to give him for Xmas."

Jake sat up. "Which reminds me." He took a small flat package from an inner pocket of his two-piece black tuxsuit. "Merry Xmas, my love." He slid the package across the white tabletop.

Hildy produced a small, square, brightly wrapped package from within her purse and passed it to him. "Same to you."

Leaning on his elbows, Jake said, "Now what about the reverend as a source of information?"

"He has a list of seventy-some possible suspected owners of Novem, Ltd." Her long tan fingers tapped on the gift package he'd given her. "And an enormous stewpot of background data, raw stuff in boxes, cartons and folders. None of it's been fed into a computer system yet. I have a copy of his list."

Jake took the faxpaper sheets she tossed on the table. "Who's the chap with the asterisk? Your next object?"

"Yep, I'll tell you about him."

"I like his name. Screwball Smith," he said. "Oh, yeah, he's the guy who runs that chain of home computer supermarkets."

" 'Nobody Is Cheaper Than Screwball Smith! And He Don't Screw Ya!' " quoted Hildy. "Even more interesting than his sales philosophy is this item. I chanced upon it when a carton fell on me and spilled over."

"Hildy, have you learned nothing from me on how to flimflam the public? Never admit to stumbling onto information. It is always the result of diligent work, dogged determination and the sort of back-breaking labor that's well worth fees of $750,000 and $1,000,000 per case." He studied the triop photo page she'd passed him.

"Reading from left to right, Jake, you see Christina Parkerhouse, Palsy Hatchbacker, Shafter 'Screwball' Smith and Professor Dickens Barrel, snapped informally while judging a Soypie Eating Contest at PMH in '98."

"You snipped this page from the Poorman's Harvard Yearbook for 1999?"

"I did. None of Lomax's investigators, the ones who've survived, have as yet explored the possible links between Novem, Big Bang and the professor," she replied. "No one else on his list ties in with Palsy and Barrel."

"So you mean to check out Screwball Smith first."

"Tomorrow morn up in Portland."

"He's open on Xmas?"

" 'Ol' SS Never Shuts! We're Dealin' 24 Hours A Day!' "

"Splendid," said Jake. "I'll be off the coast of the BajaCal Enclave tomorrow. On the private island where they produce *Captain Texas* without letup."

"Jake." She put a hand over his. "Don't get annoyed at what I am about to mention."

"I am noted for being slow to anger. Compared to me the beatific Buddha was a nervous wreck. I rarely—"

"Listen then. Whenever you get around actors and show folk, you tend to . . . Well, just don't let them distract you or flatter you so you drop your guard."

"Very sound advice," he said calmly. "I don't, however, know where you got the notion I'm vain about my God-Given acting ability. I try never to be smug about natural gifts. It's much the same with my good looks, I simply accept—"

"Even so, be careful."

"Just because a ventriloquist's dummy managed to get the drop on me recently, Hildy, that doesn't mean I'm a rube when it comes to greasepaint and—"

"Call for you, Mr. Pace." A human waiter, clad in a sarape, sombrero and white one-piece peonsuit, was carrying a portable pixphone toward their table.

A frown touched Hildy's pretty face. "Who knows we're here?"

"Nobody." He accepted the phone and stood. "I'll take it in an alcove. Back soon."

As Jake went striding to a bank of alcoves far across the room, he passed a table where a Chinese neopath and his wife were dining.

"Holy crow!" exclaimed the Chinese, dropping his forkful of enchilada. "It's him."

"Easy, Sun Yen," warned his wife.

"Xmas Eve, thousands of miles from home, and there's the infamous Jake Pace." He began shivering.

"He's merely dining out with his glamorous wife. It's a holiday and even hard-boiled private eyes have to relax now and—"

"Trouble," muttered Sun Yen. "Everywhere the Paces go, trouble follows. That time in Connecticut when we almost got incinerated and just two years ago in Manhattan when—"

"Remember what Dr. Emerzon advised. You ought not to—"

"When the shooting starts, duck under the table," advised her husband.

"How's tricks? How're you and the human skeleton? Planning to dip the old Yule log before you head back into the fray?"

"Merry Xmas, Steranko," Jake said to the image on the pixphone screen resting on the alcove shelf.

Steranko the Siphoner asked, "Aren't you amazed I was able to track you down in that greaseball bistro?"

"I'm amazed. What's up?"

"Trina Twain's real moniker is Christina Parkerhouse."

"I know."

"C'mon, Jake. It took me half a day, and most of your fee to learn that. You already knew it. How?"

"Brilliant work, dogged determination, back-breaking labor," answered Jake. "Why was it so tough to dig the information loose? Who's blocking it?"

The bald-headed siphoner shrugged. "Don't know yet. It ain't the government. Not ours anyway. I'll have more on that angle mañana. If you care to advance another $2500."

"$1500."

"Okay."

"What else have you got?"

"Maybe you already know this, too, sahib, and I'm wasting—"

"Don't sulk."

"I know where Trina is."

"That's terrific. I didn't know that."

"That's the sort of reaction I like," said Steranko. "That and cash. Trina, alias Christina, is on the moon."

"The moon?"

"That silvery orb that inspires poets and lovers, yep."

"What the hell is she doing there?"

"Nothing thus far except residing at the Sheraton-Luna. Could be, Jake, she's planning to attend the Moonport Jazz Festival, which commences in but two short days."

Jake rubbed at his chin. "Were you able to trace her back, get any idea where she's been over the last few months?"

"I did indeed. The itinerary makes fascinating reading."

"Can you tie her in with any of the locations where the Big Bang murders have taken place?"

"Not some, old buddy, but all. She was at every one, from a day before the fatal explo until a day after."

"Do me a similar check on Honey Chen and Screwball Smith."

Steranko chuckled. "You sure do rub shoulders with the great and the near great. That'll add $4500 to the tab."

"$4000."

"For a pal. Anything further?"

"What about Professor Barrel, anything on where

he might be holed up? Any links with Trina in the last year?"

"Hide nor hair of the old gent is what I ain't been able to find, Jake. I'll keep digging, throw him in for free."

"Do that."

"You going to be heading moonward?"

"Probably. But I want to visit Baja first."

"Well, bon voyage and season's greetings." The screen went black.

Jake returned to their table, almost colliding with the Chinese neopath and his wife who were scurrying out of the restaurant.

"Who was it?" asked Hildy.

"Steranko." He sat. "He's located Trina."

"Where?"

"On the moon."

Hildy said, "Going to be a lot of important folks attending the jazz festival."

"We'll need a list of them," he said. "That we can have our own Odd Jobs, Inc. computer do and save a couple thousand bucks."

"Probably have to shuttle up there, too."

"One or both of us," he said. "When you query ol' SS, find out about his travel itinerary for the past few months. For the period since the Big Bang stuff got rolling. I'll do the same for Honey Chen."

"Shall we order dinner now?"

He thought about it. "I have a suite across the street in one of the towers of the Statler-Bierce," he said. "Would you rather celebrate Xmas eve there instead of here?"

"Is this a proposition?"

"Obviously."

"Let's adjourn," Hildy said.

CHAPTER 14

————————

The voice-over announcer was saying, "Well, boys and girls, thus far it's been an exciting Xmas Day for Captain Texas and his friends. You'll remember that in yesterday's thrilling episode Captain Texas, freed from a foul Guatemalan jail after charges that he'd exposed himself at a recent Girl Scout Jamboree in this quaint little country had been proven false, encountered the mysterious Madame Scorpion, who's been turning up under such strange circumstances of late. The mysterious Madame Scorpion revealed, shortly after the captain had invited her to share his posh hotel bedroom with him, that she couldn't because she didn't believe in incest. Yes, boys and girls, Madame Scorpion is none other than Captain Texas's long lost mother. You'll recall that some months back the captain's power-mad father, Captain Texas, Sr., the lecherous solar power tycoon, admitted that he had been under the influence of powerful mind-altering drugs back when he made the particular donation to the sperm bank that resulted in the conception of our brave champion of truth and justice, Captain Texas. The captain has, ever since those startling revelations were made to him in the fever-ridden reaches of the Amazon River a few months back, been searching and seeking, in between bouts with Dr. Venial, often dubbed 'The Most Dangerous Man In The World

Today,' for his lost mother. He knew only that she wore on her ring finger a strange serpent ring which glowed mysteriously in the dark. You can imagine, boys and girls, the captain's surprise and elation when he saw that same ring glowing on the finger of the attractive mature woman he'd been planning to have a roll in the hay with. Yes, and if you'd like a ring just about like the one Captain Texas's mother wears, a ring that actually glows in the dark and contains a built-in dog whistle good for summoning at least eighty-seven different breeds of dog, then be sure to have a pen or dictabox handy at the end of today's show. There'll also be a message in code for all you members of Captain Texas's Secret Rangers. So have your decoders handy, too, boys and girls. Wellsir, back to our story. While the captain is renewing his friendship with the mother he has never known, his scoundrel of a father has succeeded in luring Leroy and Lena, the captain's two daring and loyal teen-age companions, into a brothel on the outskirts of the Tijuana Sector of Greater Los Angeles. Thereat the old tycoon offers them staggeringly large sums of money if they will perform certain disgusting sex acts with him. Let's listen. . . ."

"Gallopin' gollywogs!" exclaimed the young actor portraying Leroy. "I will not dress up in my sister's frilly lace underthings, sir."

"$100,000 and fifty shares of. . . ."

Backstage in a dim stretch of studio floor two bouncy curly-haired young men were sitting in canvas chairs on each side of Jake.

"You did very well in rehearsal," said Bill Ganpat, one of the two senior script writers.

"I know," said Jake, who was dressed in a secret agent costume.

"You have a real flair for kid opera," said Bill Tappenzee, the other senior writer. "We're really delighted you popped in when you did and agreed to fill in on this guest spot for us."

"When we heard Rance Keane had sprained his ankle at the last minute," said Ganpat, "we were really afraid we might not have anybody for today's celebrity walkon. Sometimes it's tough to get a last-minute sub down here to our private island studios in time. Then there you were."

"You're nearly as big a celeb as Rance Keane," said Tappenzee.

"I'd place myself as slightly bigger."

"Nope, we ran you through pur Personalityscope and you test out at 6.2 points behind him, but that's plenty good enough for us," said Ganpat.

Tappenzee said, "I'd like to make a teeny suggestion, Jake."

"Go ahead, Bill."

"When Honey shoots you with the lazgun, don't take quite so long to die."

Sitting up in his canvas chair, Jake said, "I died in six seconds, fellows. Considering that, I managed to put in a hell of a lot of pathos."

"Try," suggested Ganpat, "to die in four."

"In four I won't have time for the eyebrow business," Jake told him.

"It's a brilliant bit," said Tappenzee, "but we're in danger of running too long on this and the directors are bitching, Jake. So when you actually do it for the cameras, just flap your arms and flop over. If you could scrunch it into three seconds, boy, that would be even nicer."

"She could just say she shot me offstage and we don't have to—"

"We love your acting, Jake. Vidsat drama lost a real talent when you became an op," said Ganpat.

"We've got the darn serpent ring offer and a secret message to fit in today."

"This'll make my death sort of trivial," Jake explained. "Now if I had, say, a full ten seconds to expire in I—"

"Oh, gosh, don't talk like that. Ten secs would ruin us."

Tappenzee wiped his youthful face with a plyochief and frowned out at the brothel set. "Leroy's taking a heck of a long time tying Lena up with her garter belt. We're going to lose time."

"He took way too long kissing Captain Texas, Sr., too."

"Yeah, but that was poignant."

"Poignant? He and that old coot completely upstaged Lena. Lots of the kids watch us just to see Lena's tits. You know that by the mail we get. And when we gave away an authentic replica of her bra, one that also glowed in the dark, for just five dollars and three plaz Bloaties boxtops, we were flooded with orders."

"Myself I don't think her tits are as hot as they were four months ago," said Tappenzee. "If they keep slipping in the Feedback Ratings, we may have to think about replacing her."

"Why not just beef up her tits? We did that with Captain Texas's loyal companion Belphoebe Bissel of the Sexual Investigation Bureau and the faxmail was fantast—"

"She had very popular tits to begin with. And the idea of a teen-ager with tits as large as—"

"I go on in a couple minutes." Jake stood up.

"Die fast," reminded Ganpat.

Jake had arrived on the island studios off the coast of Baja California this morning at a little after nine, Southern California Conservative Time. He had a letter from Bunny Thrasher explaining he was checking out security procedures on the island for Foodopoly. When it was discovered that Rance Keane couldn't show up, Jake agreed to step in. He'd expected that would happen, since he'd bribed Keane to stay away. Acting in the highly successful kid adventure serial would put him close to Honey Chen. After the broadcast he'd see to it he had a few minutes alone with the actress. Then he'd make use of one of the several truth-getting gadgets he carried with him.

A wispy floor director nudged him. "You're on in ten seconds, Pace," he whispered. "Try to expire real fast this time."

"I'll go for the world's record."

". . . meanwhile, boys and girls," the unseen announcer was explaining, "Yasui Nekutai, the controversial lady secret agent, has traced one of Captain Texas's aides to a steambath in the Pasadena Sector of Greater Los Angeles. Quickly stripping herself naked, thus revealing the body that has dazzled the crowned heads of Europe, the Eurasian beauty, a deadly cheap Japanese import lazgun held in one shapely hand, a skimpy plyotowel hiding her erotic zone, slinks into the steam room just as Agent T14 drops his pants."

Jake had entered the steamrich set a moment before and, on cue, was dropping his trousers.

Honey Chen, playing Yasui Nekutai, entered. She was a slim girl, a pale saffron hue to her skin, and there was a sneering smile on her pretty face.

She really did, just as the announcer said, have a dazzling body. Jake studied it, getting all the way out of his trousers and reaching for a towel from the wall rack.

"Do I have the pleasure of addressing Mr. Phil Cardigan?" Honey asked.

"Why, no, my name is Reisberson," responded

Jake, delivering a rather bland line with deftness and an appealing intensity, he judged.

"Prepare to die, T14!"

Jake exclaimed, making his eyebrows rise dramatically, "How did you know who I am, you devil?"

"I know many things, fool." She whipped the prop gun from beneath her towel.

Only it wasn't a prop gun.

The distraction of her sleek naked body didn't keep Jake from realizing a real lazgun had been substituted for the one used in rehearsal.

Zizzzzle!

Jake dived to his right and rolled.

A swatch of wall was sliced away and came falling down through the bluish steam.

Offstage Ganpat was muttering, "You weren't supposed to duck. The darned scene is spoiled."

CHAPTER 15

———◆◆◆———

Screwball Smith's Portland facility consisted of eleven ranch style houses ringing a parklike area and covered with an immense plaz dome. There were sheltered landing and parking fields beyond his three-acre spread. A heavy rain was falling as Hildy brought her emerald-studded skyvan down through the grey morning. It made pinging noises on the platinum roof.

Hildy was wearing a two-piece seethru slitdress and her hair was the same exact shade as her glittering platinum-surfaced skyvan. When she slid free of the landed vehicle, long handsome legs first, a two-foot-high robot came wheeling over to her.

"Merry Xmas!" the tank-shaped mechanism chirped. "Welcome to Screwball Smith's. He's so crazy he can't be undersold. My name is Tiny Tim."

"How apt," said Hildy in a sultry voice that went with her hair. "I'm Bobbi Q and I need just absolutely oodles of home computer hardware and software to give as last minute gifts to my oodles of well-placed friends around the globe."

"Bobbi Q. Bobbi Q," Tiny Tim was chattering. "Oh! You're *the* Bobbi Q, famous celebrity and telepsetter."

"That's me, Tiny. Now can you guide me to a salesperson?"

"My memory bank doesn't include much bio on

you, Bobbi Q," admitted the little greeter 'bot, extending a metal hand and taking hold of Hildy's lovely bare arm. He led her off the landing lot and inside the main dome. "What is it exactly that you do?"

"Nothing."

"That's what you're famous for?"

"That and my incredible looks."

Tiny Tim's eye slots tilted and scanned her. "You are stunning."

"I certainly am." She squatted down beside him, bringing him to a halt. "Listen, Tiny. Since I intend to spend in the neighborhood of oodles and oodles of dollars, do you think I could get Screwball Smith himself to wait on me?"

"He rarely awakens before noon."

"Even for a famous person with oodles of money?"

"How much is an oodle?"

"Oh, let's say a million dollars at the very least."

He scanned her again. "I'll see what I can do," he said. "Meanwhile, what sort of home computer stuff do you want to inspect first?"

She stretched up, walked over beneath a decorative oak tree and glanced around at the eleven house-showrooms. "I'm going to need oodles of everything. I really was dippy, leaving all this to the very last minute."

"You certainly aren't dippy," Tiny Tim assured her. "How about some computer games for your elite friends? Over in House 6 we've got every one known to man. And at prices so low, low, low you'll think Screwball Smith is giving them away! We've got the latest version of Inquisitors & Witches, and of Rippers & Rapists and—"

"I want to stock up for my more serious pals first," Hildy told the little robot. "How about leading me to the business-oriented gadgets first?"

"That'll be House 4, right along this primrose pathway here." His little wheels snickered on the white realgravel of the path.

On many of the other paths customers were being guided by little robots similar to hers. Near a decorative birdbath a dark-haired boy of eleven suddenly pulled away from his distraught parents and threw himself into a patch of clover.

"I don't want just Rippers & Rapists! I want the Prussian Sodomists Cartridge, too! That's the one everybody else has!"

"But, Rosco," pleaded his mother, "we already bought you the Mongolian White Slavers Cartridge and the Romanian Transvestites Cartridge and—"

"Cheapskates! Poor mouthers! Just because the Prussian Sodomists Cartridge costs a measly $460 you're denying it to me! Your love is damn fragile, that's all I can say!"

Rosco's portly father took hold of one of his kicking legs. "How'd you like a Kick In The Slats Cartridge? Or maybe a Smack In The Choppers Cartridge or—"

"Gillis, don't," said his wife.

"Ah, youth," sighed Tiny Tim as he escorted Hildy up onto a brick porch. "Always yearning for the unattainable."

"I can't imagine why they just don't give the little fellow the extra $460." Hildy followed her robot into House 4.

The living room was crowded with various model computer terminals. The one nearest the doorway lit up when Hildy passed. "Hi, honey," it called out of its voxbox. "Looking for some surefire dope on the market? Or how about something good in the next race at the Jersey Dog Track? Want to toss Banx tokens or pitch—"

"This is our Tout Model," said Tiny Tim. "A bit vulgar for your friends, I'd imagine."

"Who's vulgar, you little twit?"

Hildy smiled sweetly down on the machine. "My Uncle Buford just might like this. How much?"

"Oh, you really don't want such a rowdy mech—"

"$17,000 baby," said the Tout. "For you, I might even come down to $15,500. How's about it?"

Hildy touched a finger to her lovely chin. "Seems to me that at the Psychotic Sean Computer Warehouse in Hyannis Port they have one like this for $14,000."

"Bullshit," said the Tout. "Nobody undersells Screwball Smith. Those jerkoffs in Hyannis are peddling a cheap Taiwan-2 imitation of me. It doesn't have half my functions, and less than a third of my wisecracks. For example, run your fingers over my display screen."

Hildy complied. "My! What is that?"

"Stubble. Gives you that tough guy feel. You won't get that on any Chink model."

Hildy knelt next to her little robot guide, the slit skirt exposing a length of lovely tan thigh. "TT, you promised to see if you could round up Screwball himself for me. Could you try, darling?"

"Yes, though I hate leaving you with this lunk-head."

"Aw, go piddle up a—"

"I'd really appreciate it." She planted a kiss on Tiny Tim's ball of a head.

"Very well, wait right here. The Pompous Banker Model over in the far corner is a much better buy." Giving her hand a pat, he went rolling out of the showroom.

"What a chump," observed the Tout. "Gay as a three dollar Banx chit, too."

"He's cute," said Hildy. "But, of course, so are you."

"Bet your ass I am. Let me, sister, demonstrate a few more of my—"

"Can you find out all sorts of things? I mean things that . . . you know, I might not be supposed to know."

"You're talking about shady stuff, huh? Deals that ain't exactly kosher?" His voice lowered. "I ain't supposed to do it, but just between you and me and the bedpan, sister, there ain't a damn thing I can't dig out of someplace for you."

She clapped her hands. "That's absolutely marvelous," Hildy said. "Just as a sample of what you can do . . . could you get me a look, say, at Screwball Smith's records?"

"A lead-pipe cinch, babe. Although they might get—"

"Oh, if you can't do it, that's okay. Even the model at Psychotic Sean's couldn't do some of the—"

"Shit, I can dig rings around that gook piece of junk. Try me."

Hildy narrowed one eye. "Suppose, simply to demonstrate what you claim to be able to do, you show me Screwball's travel itinerary for the past four months or so. Could you really do anything that difficult?"

"Are you kidding? That ain't tough, that's as easy as falling off a daisy wheel," the Tout assured her. "You want a printout, too, babe?"

"Might as well go first cabin."

"I can give it to you in twelve-point circus bold type, ten-point Busino extra thin, twelve-point—"

"Your choice. Something tasteful, though."

"Right you are." The terminal began producing a low humming. "This'll be a piece of . . . bonk!"

The mechanism went completely dead.

"No need to ask him, Mrs. Pace. I'll be happy to tell you where I've been."

Hildy turned and saw a freckled young man standing in the doorway.

He wore a two-piece yellow and scarlet glowsuit and a motorized polkadot bow tie. In his right hand he held a stungun.

CHAPTER 16

———••————•••———

Jake pushed the white-enameled robot aside, elbowed around the black man in the five-piece bizsuit and moved toward the door of the infirmary villa. "I'm in tip-top shape," he reiterated.

"So you say now," said the black man. "However, there's nothing to keep you from claiming whiplash, complete and total nervous collapse or acute ennui a a result of this alleged shooting accident."

"I won't."

"You ought really to lie down," urged the medical robot. "After all, the young lady shot at you with a deadly lazgun under the impression it was a prop that—"

"Ixnay," said the Negro. "The SatVid Broadcasting Network isn't admitting that Honey Chen so much as touched a real lazgun. After the tapes of the alleged incident are thoroughly studied—"

"Gentlemen," Jake told everybody in the big white room, "it's been a pleasure being served by you all. Now I must—"

"Jake," said Will Ganpat, who'd been sitting, uneasy, in a glaz slingchair, "sign the releases."

"I'm in a hurry to talk to Miss Chen," Jake said, reaching for the door. "I allowed your mechanized medic to poke and probe me. I made a statement to your insurance man. I'd—"

"You absolutely can't talk to Honey Chen now," the black insurance rep told him, catching at his arm.

"That's a point that can be debated." Jake jerked free.

"Jake," said Will Tappenzee, from a glaz sofa filled with slithering eels, "sign the releases, okay? Even though this was all an unfortunate accident, with a real gun getting mixed up with the fake ones, still—"

"We're not admitting to an accident," said the insurance man. "SVBN admits nothing until—"

"Tell you what," offered Jake. "I'll sign everything right away, if you'll let me have a five-minute chat with Honey Chen. Alone. Will?" He looked from one writer to the other.

"Don't see why not, Jake. After—"

"No," cut in the insurance man. "Suppose he persuades that quiff to admit she—"

"Eli, we have the whole damn thing on tape," said Tappenzee. "96,000,000 loyal viewers around the world saw it happen. So—"

"By the way, Jake," said Ganpat, "you may have to hop back later in the week and be Agent T14 again. Since you didn't get properly stunned this time."

Tappenzee said, "It played pretty well, though. The Feedback indicates 76 percent of the kids were Pleased and Thrilled by her cutting a monumental chunk out of the darn wall and nearly slicing Jake into—"

"Ixnay, ixnay. We're not admitting anything was sliced or—"

"Five minutes with Honey," said Jake, fishing an electropen out of a pocket. "Has nothing to do with her using a so-called real gun to allegedly take a shot at me."

"Okay by me." Ganpat got up.

"Okay by me." Tappenzee got up.

"Gentlemen, I don't know if SVBN can allow—"

"We can." Ganpat took all the release forms from the insurance man and thrust them at Jake.

"Vacation," said Tappenzee, remembering.

"She'll be back in time to attempt to feed Lena and Leroy to the sludge-eating bacteria in next week's exciting episodes, though," added Ganpat.

The three of them were in the enormous living room of Honey Chen's private villa on the ocean-facing side of the island.

Jake was prowling, poking at piles of faxmags, kicking into sprawls of discarded lingerie. "Know where she's going to vacation?"

"You're not planning to chase after her? That really must've been an accident."

"We have no idea how a real gun got mixed up with the props, Jake."

"But we're sure as heck going to investigate."

"You bet."

Grinning bleakly, Jake told them, "That's a damn good impersonation of Leroy and Lena."

"Gee, Jake, don't go making fun of—"

"The moon," said Jake. "Right?"

"What?"

"That's where Honey Chen is going to spend her latest vacation from *Captain Texas*," amplified Jake as he continued to prowl the room.

There was a faint growling sound coming from some other room.

He went in search of it.

"Well . . ." said Ganpat, following.

"Well," said Tappenzee, following.

"She's probably developed a sudden interest in jazz and doesn't want to miss the Moonport Jazz Festival."

Jake side-stepped into the room that was producing the small noise.

"She's always been deeply interested in jazz," said Ganpat. "Look there on her bedroom wall is a triop gloposter of Lafcadio Latterly."

"Impressive, convincing." Genuflecting beside the floatbed, Jake nudged it aside with one shoulder.

The dispozhole under the bed hadn't been able to digest the last few pieces of paper stuffed into it and was making a metallic gagging sound.

Carefully Jake rescued the three balls of crumpled faxpaper. He stood and smoothed them out. One was a confirm slip for a Moonshuttle flight departing this afternoon from the GLA Spaceport, one was a scrawled memo from Will Ganpat urging Honey to be "more insidious if you can," and the final paper that had escaped destruction had a string of numbers hastily scribbled across it.

"(CT6) 17*25/2*21*16*25/2/10*21*23*25/5*25* 25*10*3*8*1/3*8/13*21/15*8*14*3*6/21*26*14*25* 12/7*9*9*8/13*13," the complete message read.

"Are those clues to anything, Jake?" inquired Tappenzee.

After scanning the departed actress's bedroom, Jake moved out into the hall. "How many codes are there on the Captain Texas decoder?"

"Gee, you really are taking an interest in the show," said Ganpat while he and his partner trailed Jake back into the living room.

"Eight codes is the answer," said Tappenzee. "You set the dingus for any number from one to eight and that lines up the letters and numbers in diff—"

"I'd like undiluted silence for a few minutes," requested Jake. He dropped into a snugchair that faced the bright calm Pacific.

"Sure." Ganpat sat, tenatively, on the edge of a swingsofa.

Tappenzee settled near him. "You going to go over the events of today in your mind to—"

"Hush," advised Jake, digging out the decoder that had originally been among the stuff Bullet Benton had carted off from Poorman's Harvard.

Using the decoder and his electropen, he got the message unraveled in just under five minutes.

It said, "We have H. Pace. Keeping in S.A. until after Moon. S.S."

Jake said, "Damn."

CHAPTER 17

Hildy could see down through the seethru floor, quite easily since she was sprawled out on it with her arms strapped behind her, and watch the big processing plant at work. Large quantities of nunca beans were being trucked in and converted, by way of a complex and noisy method, into fuel oil. Each pale green truck had the Newoyl sign on its sides and top. Out beyond one of the open doorways of the factory she saw a wide road that came cutting through the dense jungle.

"South America someplace," she told herself. "And, damn it, Jake has no idea where I am."

Wiggling, she got into a sideways position and scrutinized more thoroughly the room she'd awakened in some five or so minutes ago.

There was nothing much to see. Grey plaz walls, one door with no inside handle, no windows. Not a single piece of furniture, nothing much in the way of dust.

Whoever'd tossed her in here had taken her shoes, and along with them the miniature escape kit she carried in a heel compartment.

The door hummed for a few seconds, then slid open.

Screwball Smith, smiling, came in. Accompanying him were a thick-set young man and a lean silver-haired young woman. Smith was still decked out in yellow and scarlet. Both the others wore glojeans.

"I never apologize," said Smith, crossing the room and stopping beside the sprawled Hildy. "You and your husband intruded, you got hurt. That's the way things go."

"Very practical and businesslike," said Hildy. "You'd be surprised how few murderers are."

"I never get angry either, so don't waste time needling me, Mrs. Pace." He sat down, crosslegged, on the floor. "Any idea where you are?"

"Newoyl has seven plants in South America to process nunca beans. This is one of them."

"Actually we now have nine. You're in the newest one, near our plantation in the wilds of Panazuela."

"Business is picking up," said Hildy.

"We've been arranging things so it would," Smith said, his smile broadening.

"And what are you going to arrange for me?"

"I'm never moved by emotional displays either," he told her. "So don't bother sobbing, screaming and pleading when I inform you we're going to be killing you."

Nodding, Hildy said, "When?"

"Not until I return."

"From the moon?"

He laughed. "Very good, Mrs. Pace." Smith got to his feet. "You'll be questioned some while I'm away. When I get back, in about four days' time, I'll arrange your death."

Hildy said, "You're part of Novem."

"Yes." He tapped the side of his skull with a forefinger and produced a faint metallic *bong*. "There are five of us. Should've been six, but we could never convince Palsy to join with us. We left her alone until she decided to contact Odd Jobs, Inc."

"Then you killed her."

"We felt some regret there, since she had one of the prof's implants and might've been useful." He shrugged his checkered shoulders. "But we'd given her more than enough chances and she remained stubborn. Actually, as you know, the five of us have done quite well without her."

"Don't feel bad about Palsy, she obviously brought it on herself by defying you."

"Both you and your husband have reputations for being wiseasses. I can't say I enjoy that sort of thing."

"Gallows humor," Hildy said. "Do forgive me."

Smith gestured for the other two to join him. "Mrs. Pace, these folks'll be looking after you while I'm gone. Frat McGinty, this is Mrs. Hildy Pace."

The chunky McGinty grunted. "So can I, SS?"

"Not now, Frat."

"Shit, I don't see why not." He'd slid a Teflon-coated machete out from under his tunic.

"Because, asshole, I don't want her all bloodied up before Dr. Bensen sees her."

McGinty said, "I'd only just slice her on the bottoms of her feet, SS, and out of the way places like that. I won't spoil her any. Shit, you're going to kill her anyhow eventually."

"After Dr. Bensen is through with his interrogation sessions."

"Oh, sure, but she'll be in a coma by then probably," complained McGinty, rubbing his machete blade along the leg of his tight-fitting glojeans. "It's nowhere near as much fun when you can't hear her scream."

"Remember how you got in trouble back at PMH, Frat?" Smith reminded, taking hold of his associate's arm.

"Yeah, but that dame was a full prof and I sliced

her up with a rare Druid knife from the Boston Museum of—"

"You'll leave Mrs. Pace alone," said Smith evenly.

"Shit."

Smith said, "And this, Mrs. Pace, is Lady Loo Lepper, the famous British socialite you've no doubt heard about via the mass media."

"Who?" asked Hildy.

"Droll," said the platinum-haired girl, kicking Hildy in the ribs.

"I don't want you spoiling her either," warned Smith.

"Really, Smitty, old bean, you're a royal pain in the toke," observed Lady Loo. "I mean, I sometimes wonder why I left wealth and position in jolly old England for a life of nastiness among such swine as you and the Novem crew."

"You're to guard her and that's all, Lady Loo."

After kicking Hildy once again, Lady Loo strolled away to lean against the far wall. "It's so bloody dull here, Smitty, old bean. Then when the chance for a bit of fun comes up, you start acting like a preacher."

Smith squatted next to Hildy. "I wanted you to meet the folks who'll be looking after you," he said, smiling broadly. "Bye for now."

Frat McGinty said, "Ouch!"

"Whatever is the matter, old bean?" asked Lady Loo.

They were both lounging on the broad, shady veranda of the staff house, facing a panorama of sun-drenched jungle.

"I cut my damn finger," Frat replied.

"Well, that's better than nothing."

After wrapping a plyochief around his left forefinger, Frat rested his machete across his lap. "Screwball's been gone a couple hours and Dr. Bensen won't be here until nightfall. We could fool around with that redheaded bimbo for a while and nobody'd know."

Lady Loo ran long sharp-edged fingers through her silvery hair and slumped farther down in her neorattan chair. "We'd better not, love," she sighed. "I don't really fancy crossing Screwball. Just yet."

"I still say I could slice her in . . . Jumpin' jellybeans!" He popped to his feet, dropping his machete and snatching a kilgun from his holster.

"Whatever is . . ." The silver-haired young woman turned to look in the direction her companion was staring.

A small man with an improbable head of straw-color hair had come stumbling out of the green jungle. He was making his staggering way toward them, with the seemingly unconscious body of a near naked man over his shoulders.

Cautiously, McGinty went clomping down the wooden steps with his gun at the ready. "Who the frap are you?"

"I've found him!" exclaimed the tottering man in a cracked and thirsty voice. "Yes, yes, man, I have actually found him!"

"When did you lose him?" inquired Lady Loo, standing to lean on the veranda rail.

"This may well be," continued the straw-haired man, "the major find of the 21st century, and, when you consider the century is only a few years old, you'll realize just how—"

"There's something important about that tacky-looking gink?" McGinty gestured at the long lean nearly naked man.

"Permit me to introduce myself. I am Dr. Wilhelm

Black-Schwartz," said Steranko the Siphoner. "Of the prestigious Burroughs Foundation."

"And who's your friend?" asked Lady Loo.

"Why, my dear child," said Steranko as he carried his burden up into the shade near her, "this is the fabled Wild Man of Panazuela."

"Never heard of him." McGinty came climbing back up the steps.

"Originally he was known as the Wild Boy of Panazuela." Steranko dumped Jake down on the planks. "He's matured considerably since then."

"He certainly has, old bean," observed Lady Loo.

Steranko rubbed his grimy hands together. "Do either of you realize what this means? Here you see a feral man, a creature who's grown up entirely away from civilization, a—"

"Doesn't matter what he is," cut in McGinty. "You can't dump him here."

"But, my dear sir. . . ." Steranko swayed, touched his stained forehead and took several tottering steps backward. He collapsed into a neorattan sofa. "You must forgive me, I've been nearly a week without food. After I ate the last porter, it's been very—"

"You've been lost in the jungle?" asked Lady Loo, eyes on the sprawled Jake.

"For endless weeks," moaned the siphoner.

Jake groaned. He had a tangled, matted head of long dark hair and wore a loincloth made of badly tanned animal skin. There was a necklace of monkey teeth around his neck.

Lady Loo poked him with her foot. "Whyever is he in this terrible shape?"

"I have to keep stunning the creature." Steranko casually took a stungun from an inner pocket of his tan two-piece bushsuit. "Otherwise he attacks and bites." He started to roll up a sleeve. "I'll show you the marks he made in my—"

"Watch where you're waving that gun," suggested McGinty.

Jake opened his eyes and sat up. "Unk," he said.

Steranko said, "He speaks neither English, Spanish nor any Indian tongue."

"So I noticed," said Lady Loo.

Jake gazed up at her, suspicion and then elation showing on his savage face. "Unk unk!" he exclaimed, making a grab for her ankle.

"That won't do," said Steranko, raising the stungun.

Zzzzzummmmmmm!

"Goodness me," said Steranko, frowning at the stunner in his hand. "I seem to have missed and hit your colleague, young lady."

Thunk!

McGinty had toppled over onto his face, his kilgun skating away into deep shadows.

"You blooming halfwit!" Lady Loo cried. "You've gone and ... oh!"

Jake clamped a tiny silver disc onto her calf. He scrambled up, saying, "Sit down and be quiet."

"You can stuff ... that is ... yes, guv." Her eyes went round and staring as the control bug took her over.

Jake scooped up the kilgun and the machete. "How many guards around this place?"

"Fifteen," she replied in a dead voice. "In fact, two of them should have stopped you before you got anywhere near this part of—"

"They're in snoozeland," said Steranko, chuckling. "Who else is in the main house here?"

"No one."

Bending, the siphoner took hold of the truly unconscious Frat McGinty. He dragged him, with ease, into the house and came quickly back outside. "Proceed, Jake."

"Is Screwball here?"

"No, guv."

"Where is he?"

"En route to the moon."

Jake nodded, savage locks of hair flapping. "Okay, and where is Hildy Pace?"

"In an interrogation room."

"Whereabouts?"

"Over the factory."

Jake said, "You'll take us there."

"I will."

"Who is Novem going to kill next?"

"I don't know."

Steranko urged, "Let's get moving, Jake."

"Lead us to Hildy now." He took hold of the young woman's arm.

She stood. "This way, guv." Lady Loo, moving a bit stiffly, descended the steps into the yellow glare of the afternoon.

"We've done terrifically thus far," said Steranko as he tagged along.

"And Hildy says I can't act." Jake grinned and scratched his bare chest.

CHAPTER 18

◆━━━◆◆◆━━━◆

Jake made another circuit of their compartment. "I think I'm right," he said.

Hildy, once again herself, glanced out the multi-layered window at the crisp darkness the Moon-shuttle was passing through. "Backtrack a bit before we get to Professor Barrel and the kids from the class of '99," she requested. "Explain, in a bit more detail, how you and Steranko located me in the wilds of Panazuela."

Sitting down opposite her on the tan neoleather seat, he grinned. "Was I or was I not a convincing wild man?"

"If it weren't for the fact I know your unclothed body fairly well, you'd have fooled even me. But how—"

"I intercepted a code message Screwball Smith sent to Honey Chen."

"How'd you do that?"

"Dogged detective work," he answered.

"And the message told you exactly where I was being held?"

"Nope, it only said you'd be in South America until after the moon festivities."

She shivered, hugging herself. "They meant to kill me, Jake."

"Yeah, I know." He crossed the small tan compartment to sit beside her. "I got Steranko to use his illegal tapping equipment to check on the comings and goings between Portland and the Newoyl plants in Latin America."

"And that gave you the Panazuela location."

"Actually we only narrowed it down to Panazuela and Ereguay," he admitted. "Before we hit your factory, we'd pulled the same act over in Ereguay. Went over pretty well there, too."

"I'm glad you didn't stop to take bows and do encores. The lad named Frat was intent on slicing me up some."

Jake said, "Neither Frat nor Lady Loo know much about the inner workings of Novem. All they gave us is the fact that something is planned for the moon during the jazz festival."

"Screwball Smith'll be there."

"So will Honey Chen. Trina is already there."

"It looks like—"

Tap! Tap! Tap!

Jake moved to the door, flicked the spyhole knob. "It's Steranko," he announced.

"I still don't see why we're dragging him along, and at first-class rates."

"He helped save your life, my dear."

"I'm eternally grateful, but that doesn't make him the sort of traveling compan—"

Tap! Tap! Tap! Tap!

"C'mon, c'mon, open wide. I need sanctuary," said the siphoner on the other side of the door.

Jake admitted him. "Trouble?"

Although Steranko had donned a two-piece yellow suit, he'd retained the straw-color wig that went with his earlier impersonation. His face was flushed at the

moment. "I am used to eccentricities," he said, hurrying into the compartment and shutting the door with
an elbow. "But I sure don't go in for that sort of
thing."

"What sort of thing?"

"Some of the musicians heading for the moon are
sharing this shuttle flight with us," he explained, sitting, panting. "I was in the men's room when this per-
fectly decent looking chap entered and stepped into a
cubicle. Intent on combing my wig . . . I don't, you
know, usually travel with hair and this is something of
a diverting novelty . . . intent of combing my wig, I
didn't notice him until he'd emerged. Only now he
was a lady with long blond hair."

"He's put on a wig, too?" asked Hildy.

"No, he switched," said the flustered Steranko. "I
realized I was encountering a member of Switchit
McBernie's All Girl-All Boy Orchestra. The whole
blooming ensemble is made up of switchsexuals. The
one I met is Max-Maxine and His/Her Magic Violin."

Jake laughed. "Did they pursue you?"

"I gave him the slip, and ran for your compartment."

"You can hide here for a spell," Jake told him.
"We'll dock on the moon in about six hours."

Hildy eyed the siphoner. "You won't have to stay
here six hours, will you? Your plight isn't that serious."

"I'd rather kiss a violinist than spend six hours with
you, Skinny."

Hildy smiled. "You're returning to your normal
self, meaning the shock is subsiding."

Scratching at his wig, Steranko asked, "Did I inter-
rupt a family squabble? Go right ahead on with it,
don't mind my presence."

"Jake and I were discussing the Big Bang case," Hildy informed him. "Oh, and I do appreciate your leaving that electronic sinkhole of yours, Steranko, and coming out into the real world to help save me."

"I was just about the whole rescue mission," he said, tapping his chest. "Jake was playing Sleeping Beauty most of the time. And, geez, what an implausible wild man. 'Ung, ung,' is all he could think to say. I was scared they'd tumble to his feeble—"

"Unk unk," corrected Jake.

Twining his fingers together, Steranko asked, "Have you told the missus about the possible targets?"

"Was just about to introduce the topic," said Jake.

"Targets plural?" asked his wife.

"There are two probable targets we know of," said Jake.

"There are two and that's it *period*," put in the siphoner. "I did my usual thorough job on this. There's not going to be anybody else on the moon who qualifies."

"The most likely target for the Big Bang gang is Tilda Host," said Jake, settling down next to Hildy. "She's Chairman of the Board of Sinoil, Ltd."

"They make fuel oil out of jojoba beans," said Hildy. "Meaning they compete with Newoyl."

"There's also a merger in the works with another big synthetic oil outfit," added Steranko. "Should something happen to the old squack that'd fall through. Another plus for Newoyl and Novem."

Jake said, "The other candidate is Bonny Prince Freddy of the Portugal Annex. There are rumors of rich untapped real oil deposits beneath most of his little country. His papa, Bonny King Freddy, is terminally goofy and the prince runs the country."

Folding her arms under her breasts, Hildy gazed

out into space. "They might be going for both of them."

"So far they've been doing one at a time," said Jake, "although that doesn't necessarily mean they can't change their pattern."

"Whatever they plan, they may go for their target during a session of the festival," she said. "That can mean maybe a thousand innocent people going at the same time that—"

"Two hundred and twenty-six with one blow is their record thus far."

"I don't like this one, Jake," she shook her head. "We've dealt with some wretched people before, like Adolph Hibbler and Dr. Patchwork, but these kids . . . do you know who they all are yet?"

Jake nodded at Steranko the Siphoner. "We've come up with, by checking travel patterns and lists of Poorman's Harvard grads, a list of five."

"I assume Screwball Smith's name is near the top."

Steranko recited, "Screwball Smith, Christina Parkerhouse (DBA Trina Twain), Honey Chen, Lafcadio Latterly and Derrick Thrasher."

"Thrasher of the Foodopoly clan?"

"A black sheep cousin of Bunny Thrasher's, graduated with the Class of '99," filled in Jake.

Hildy frowned. "What about Professor Barrel? Isn't he the mastermind behind this all?"

"He's stone cold dead," said Steranko. "Has been since his so-called flit from PMH last year. If the Federal Police Agency cops had the sort of facilities I have, they'd have discovered the fact months ago."

"Is that true, Jake?"

He said, "Steranko went through untold numbers of morgue records, potters field archives, missing persons reports and a stewpot of other stuff."

"The prof died in a faked pedramp accident in Cuba-3 approximately two and a half weeks after he left the Boston area," the siphoner said. "They'd done a quickie ID wipe on the poor bastard and he was cremated as a John Doe. It is absolutely Dickens Barrel, even though we maybe can't prove it from his alleged ashes at this point."

"Why kill him?" Hildy asked.

"Easier for them," said Jake. "They'd been working on this idea ever since that accident back in school, when they blew up part of the building. Soon as they were ready to move, the Novem bunch didn't want Barrel around."

"Even if he talked, they—"

"Wasn't just that, Hildy. I think they were afraid he'd be able to come up with a way to stop them."

Hildy said, "Did he leave any notes, any records on how you might—"

"Nothing we've been able to dig out so far," replied Jake. "But there's got to be some way to turn off those gadgets implanted in their noggins."

"A nice blast with a kilgun would do the trick," suggested Steranko.

Hildy tapped her fingertips on her knee. "While I was a guest of Screwball Smith's," she said, "he talked about killing me, but—"

"That son of a bitch," said Jake.

"But he never threatened an explosion," she concluded. "One of them alone can't do it, isn't that it, Jake? They have to work as a team, it's a synergistic setup. Sure, because he said something about never being able to get Palsy to work with them."

"Yep, they have to do it in tandem." Jake stood. "That must be something they learned from the first, unintended, explosion. It takes the whole group for a Big Bang."

"Then if we can keep them apart," Hildy said, "they—"

"Hell," said Steranko, "for all we know they're already joining hands up on the moon this very minute."

CHAPTER 19

————••————

The very old woman dabbed perfume behind her tin ear. This caused her fur-trimmed dressing gown to sprawl open and reveal the blend of flesh, metal and wires that was her chest. "No peeking, you rascal," she rattled.

The extremely blond young man reclining on the thermorug beside her glaz chair snickered. Then he reached up to tweak her surviving breast. "Can't help it, doll baby."

Struggling to keep her nose from wrinkling, Hildy said, "Mrs. Host, you really are in danger."

Tilda Host dabbed perfume behind her flesh ear, squinting at the image of her ancient face that the floating mirror showed her. "Lon, who did this young lady say she was?"

Lon Wranger yawned, gave a catlike stretch and reached into a hip pocket of his glojeans. He withdrew the business card. "Odd Jobs, Inc.," he read.

"Who are they?"

"We're private investigators." Hildy crossed the boudoir section of the hotel suite toward the old Sinoil tycoon. "Working for the United States Government on this—"

"I've never heard of you. Further . . . Oh, Lon, don't be a naughty boy."

133

"Can't control myself, doll baby." He'd commenced licking at her aluminum foot.

"Mrs. Host, it's fairly certain an attempt on your life will—"

"You're just trying to upset her," accused Wranger, rising up on one elbow and glaring at Hildy. "Her poor plaz ear can't stand that, really."

"She probably can't stand an explosion either," Hildy told the blond boy. "That's why you have to leave the moon before—"

"Where's my eye?" The old woman was patting the cluttered floating vanity table with her gnarled hands.

"Silly, you're wearing both your lovely eyes."

"I mean the emerald one," said Tilda Host.

Wranger pursed his lips. "That's in the hotel safe, angel cakes. Along with your platinum leg."

"But I want to wear it." With a silver suction tool she removed the glaz eye that had filled her left socket. "If you have nice eyes, you ought to show them."

"I know, doll baby, but this is a jazz festival we're attending," Wranger reminded. "Someone might rob you."

"I have bodyguards to prevent that and . . . young woman, why are you still here?"

"To persuade you to leave. Right away," said Hildy. "Otherwise you're going to be the next Big Bang victim."

"Don't keep talking like that," warned Wranger, easing up and slipping a protective arm around the old woman's narrow shoulders. "You're upsetting angel cakes."

Tilda Host asked, "What's she babbling about, Lon?"

"Nothing. Pay no attention, doll baby." He scowled at Hildy. "You don't have any proof, do you?"

"Nothing I can show you, but you'll have to trust us when—"

"I want to see the festival," insisted the old woman. "All my favorites are appearing." She patted Wranger's tan young hand with copper fingers. "Who are my favorites, dear?"

He slid a plazpaper advance program out of a hip pocket. "Tonight we'll be catching Zootz Zankowitz and His Cyborg Swingers, plus—"

"Is he the one with the tenor saxophone implanted in his—"

"No, no, apple dumpling, that's Bix Briggs. We'll catch him and his Big Brass Band tomorrow afternoon in Jazz Pavilion 2."

"Who else, hon? Doesn't he have an exciting voice?"

"Listen, please," said Hildy, advancing toward Tilda Host. "An outfit called Novem is—"

"Tomorrow it's Switchit McBernie and His All Girl-All Boy Orchestra, Lafcadio Latterly and His Latter Day Saints," read Wranger. "Robotman and His Non-Human Jug Band. Jelly Roll Morton and His Red Hot Peppers. That's the Jazz Simulacra group from New Oreleans. Then—"

"Blowing up is going to give your business rivals a real advantage, Mrs. Host."

"Lon, I'm vacationing. I don't want to hear a single word about business," complained the old woman. "Send this gawky girl away."

After returning the program to his pocket, Wranger edged over to take hold of Hildy's arm. "If you have any proof of real trouble, dear lady, go to the Moon Authority Police. Don't come intruding in here anymore."

"You'll go blooey, too," Hildy said, allowing him to escort her to a door. "That's the pattern, angel cakes."

"Nonsense." He pushed her out into the corridor.

The honey-blonde young woman said, "Oh, shoot!" Jake picked up her dictabox again, returned it to her shapely lap. "This really is an emergency situation, Miss . . ."

Her eyes widened. "Darnation, don't you actually know who I am?"

"Private secretary to the Director of the Moonport Jazz Festival." He began pacing the large oval reception room.

"No, heckbeck, I mean my identity. I'm celebrated, besides being a crackerjack secretary."

He was gazing out the seethru wall at the nest of jazz pavilions spread out far below. Lightsigns were being strung up and tested over the half dozen separate auditorium domes; vendors were assembling souvenir and refreshment stands; a fat lady was inflating lifesize Switchit McBernie balloons with a gazgun. "If I guess right about who you are," he said, turning and favoring the pretty blonde with a grim grin, "will you go in and tell your boss this is urgent?"

"I have to take down the nature of you and your business first on this dingdang machine. That prints up a memo that the telebox zips into him." She set the somewhat dented dictation machine on her tin desk. "Here. Maybe this'll give you a hint." After clearing her pretty throat, she put both hands behind her shapely back. "Pretend I'm tied up."

"Ah, yes." Jake snapped his fingers. "You're Taffeta Bearslair. Now then, tell Colonel Bunch that—"

"I was Submissive Slave Centerfold of the Year in *Docile* in 2002," she said, smiling at him. "Probably you didn't recognize me right off without my chains."

"And the wisp of black lace nightie." He came close to her desk. "Look, somebody is going to make an assassination try at the festival. Maybe at the first session tonight. The colonel is going to have to—"

"Talk a bit slower if you can," she requested. "I'll tell you why I'm working as a private secretary at the present moment and not pursuing my career as one of the top masochist models on Earth. I woke up one morning a few months ago and I felt very dominant all of a sudden. 'Heckbeck, Taffeta,' I said, addressing myself while I proceeded to untie the realeather bonds I usually sleep in, 'you ought to be more assertive. Stop letting people tie you up and work you over with whips.' Maybe it was because I had just read Dr. Rocky Sarantonio's wonderful faxbook on assertiveness, entitled *How'd You Like A Punch In The Nose?* Wellsir, I leaped out of my bed of nails, shed my filmy black nightie and—"

"Taffeta," said Jake, a shade impatiently, "I'm going to assert myself now." He skirted her tin desk, sprinted across the white linofloor and pushed the door marked *Col. Kissin' Jim Bunch PRIVATE.*

"Oh, darnation. I'm still being trampled over by folks."

Bunch was in his office, a tall raw-boned man in a two-piece grey bizsuit. There was no desk in the vast octagonal room. Only a single glaz chair near the farthest wall. Bunch was in that chair, toying with a small self-waving Moonport Jazz Festival pennant. "This thing flaps far too fast, Taff . . . Sir, what causes you to come charging into my sanctum?"

"I'm Jake Pace of Odd Jobs, Inc., and—"

"Oh really? The notorious PI, eh?" said Bunch. "I received no memo from my stunning secretary announcing your—"

"You've heard of the Big Bang Murders, haven't you?"

"Who hasn't? Any well-read, well-viewed citizen of—"

"The people responsible are on the moon, planning a new murder."

Bunch watched his rapidly waving pennant for a few seconds. "My goodness," he said finally.

Jake stalked over to him. "Okay, here's the situation," he said. "They are going to knock off either Tilda Host or Bonny Prince Freddy, both of whom are attending concerts at your festival tonight. What you have to do is postpone the concerts until we—"

"Wouldn't it be infinitely simpler, old man, to send Mrs. Host and the prince packing, get them off the moon entirely?"

"It would," agreed Jake. "Unfortunately the prince is wooing Wee Bettsi Bierstadt, the freefal vocalist with the Zootz Zankowitz group. He can't be—I just tried—persuaded to depart. Neither can Tilda Host."

The colonel said, "You are the same chap who murdered that singer down in Chicago, are you not?"

"I'm the chap falsely accused."

"Um." Bunch reached into his tunic. "Just two and one half hours ago, Mr. Pace, I received a very interesting telegram." He held up a rectangle of pale yellow faxpaper. "From the Federal Police Agency of the United States on Earth. I shall now read it to you in its entirety. 'Believe crazed sex killer known as Jake Pace headed your way Stop Pay no attention to his ravings Stop Will arrive on moon soonest myself to look after him Stop FPA and your Government appreciate any effort you make to give this notorious habitual criminal bad cess Stop Copies of this urgent message also going to Moon Authority Police and Lunar Bureau of Investigation Stop Signed—'"

"Bullet Benton," said Jake.

Hildy, a plyotowel wrapped around her just washed auburn hair, crossed the living room of their suite in the Statler-Moon and seated herself in a neosilk slingchair.

"Get out of phone range," suggested Jake over his shoulder. He was, slightly hunched, stationed in the pixphone alcove. "I don't want everybody in the Department of Security being distracted by visions of my naked wife."

"I am sedately clothed." She adjusted the green towel around her torso.

"Well, at least uncross your legs. You look naked in that pose."

"I never pose, Jake. You're the actor in the family. While I—"

"Ready with your call to DC," announced the phone in a falsetto voice.

Secretary Strump's face was less pugnacious, there were sags of shadow under his eyes. "Try not calling me collect next time, Jake," he commenced. "The Budget Office is bitching about—"

"There's going to be a Big Bang murder here," Jake told the man on the phone screen. "Tonight. Maybe two murders."

"Is that why you're on the moon?" asked the Secretary of Security. "I didn't believe the toll charges they quoted me until—"

"I can't get any cooperation from the local law," Jake went on. "Here's what you have to do, and why. The Big Bang gang is on the moon. We know they're going after either Tilda Host or Bonny Prince Freddy. Both of those nitwits will be attending the jazz festival tonight. If there's an explosion, thousands of people will die along with—"

"Never cared much for jazz. Polka music is my—"

"Thanks to Bullet Benton, my standing on the moon isn't at an all-time high," Jake told the cabinet member. "But we have to postpone the concerts and evacuate the targets' hotels. Right now. Then, while Hildy and I are tracking down—"

"Can't you just tell these alleged targets to scram? That would—"

"Strump, we did that," said Jake, "to no avail."

"Things," said the chunky secretary, slumping some in his desk chair, "things are not going smoothly hereabouts. I, at your suggestion, ran a new, double-strength, seccheck. After all, who is better qualified than the Secretary of Security to check the security of his very own—"

"What's the point of this discourse?"

"There was a leak in the organization. And I found it," said Strump, a look of weary satisfaction on his face. "A young fellow with an excellent background dossier is who it turned out to be. He got all A's in his classes at—"

"Poorman's Harvard," said Jake. "Now, Strump, get busy on—"

"How'd you know that?"

"Dogged detective work," said Hildy.

The secretary leaned to his left. "Oh, hello there, Hildy. How are you? Are you sitting there naked?"

"Nope."

"From here it looks as though—"

"I'm happy you found the spy," cut in Jake. "But we have to take action about the situation up here on—"

"I haven't yet told you all the problems besetting me," said Secretary Strump. "You see, in order to interfere with any law organization on the moon . . . this all goes back to the OffEarth Intrusion Act of

2001 and the Greim-Cosgrove Bill . . . At any rate, Jake, I need a presidential okay before I can do anything at all."

"Get it."

"Would that it were that simple," sighed the secretary. "This is confidential, I don't want the *Intruder* or *Mammon* or vidshows like *Good Morning, White America* to get hold of this, but Mike and Ike . . . well, they've had a little tiff. Actually it was over a squabble the First Ladies had as to who sleeps on which side of the official White House waterbed in—"

"What does all this domestic stuff have to do with your getting those identical nitwits to authorize you to—"

"They aren't speaking," explained Strump. "Mike isn't speaking to Ike, Ike isn't speaking to Mike. Consequently, they won't agree on anything and nobody can get them to sign a damn thing."

"So get the White House name-signing robot to do it."

"No, Jake, that's only for letters to school children, minor legislations and—"

"Never mind," Jake said evenly. "We'll handle it all from here."

"How?"

"We'll go out and catch the damned assassins before they get together and kill anyone," he said.

CHAPTER 20

Steranko came through the doorway, trailing loose wires and waving a long length of printout paper. "I've got something good," he announced.

Closing the suite door, Jake asked, "Such as?"

"The location of the gang, for one thing." He shook threads of yellow and blue wire off his foot. "Stepped in one of my makeshift databoxes in my haste to rush up here."

Hildy, wearing a two-piece slaxsuit and sitting in a slingchair, inquired, "Is that why we brought him along, Jake?"

Jake nodded. "He's set up a temporary siphoning station down in his suite."

"You call that a suite? Why, you have to step out into the hall to change—"

"What have you got?" Jake led the bald young man across the room, placed him in a spunglaz chair. "Give us details."

"Christina Parkerhouse, alias Trina Twain and Woodrow, no longer resides at the Sheration-Luna."

"That we already knew," reminded Jake. "I figured they'd go underground once they knew we were heading here."

"Use your ears for a moment and not your bazoo," advised Steranko the Siphoner. "By using the ingenious portable tapping equipment I lugged up here, plus some brilliantly improvised dohickies, I have traced the whole kaboodle to their lair."

"Terrific." Jake grinned.

Steranko glanced over at Hildy. "Do I hear similar terms of approbation from the distaff, Skinny?"

"Terrific," she said.

"Screwball Smith," proceeded the information bootlegger, "rented a chalet in a fashionable suburb of Moonport, acquiring same via a labyrinthine system of cover names and circumlocutions. The address is 919 Armstrong Lane, a very posh locale."

Hildy stood. "They're all there?"

"From checking out shuttle arrivals, baggage transportation and transfer, I can now state that Screwball Smith, Honey Chen, Christina-Trina and Derrick 'Black Sheep' Thrasher are all snug within the chalet."

"What about Lafcadio Latterly?" asked Jake.

Steranko flipped a festival program from out of a pocket of his cocoa suit. "There has been a last-minute change in the agenda of tonight's perf," he said. "Scratch Zootz Zankowitz and add Lafcadio L."

Jake rubbed his chin. "Then they won't try anything tonight," he said.

"Unless they can whip up an explosion without LL," said the siphoner.

"But even if they could do that, they won't blow him up along with their targets."

Hildy said, "There's another possibility, Jake."

"Which is?"

"Well, we know they can control the limits of the area they want to explode," she said. "They could be joining Lafcadio at the festival, planning to do their trick there. You know, they gather at a given spot and blow up everything a couple hundred yards off and beyond."

"That's a possibility, since we don't know how close to a target they usually get."

Rattling his collection of printout paper, Steranko said, "I don't think tonight's the night, folks. Mainly because the gang is having a party this eve, commencing any minute."

Hildy asked him, "How do you know that?"

"A catering service, entirely robot-staffed, has been hired to deliver booze and fancy chow no later than six tonight to the chalet," he said. "My guess is, the class of '99 plans to do a bit of celebrating prior to their next killing."

"Maybe," said Jake thoughtfully. "Latterly's being put on at a new and unexpected time could've caused a postponement."

"That gives me time to try again on the targets," said Hildy.

"Tilda Host won't—"

"I was thinking of working on Bonny Prince Freddy," his wife said. "Any man who thinks Wee Bettsi Bierstadt is attractive ought to find me overwhelming."

Jake's left eye narrowed as he looked at her. "This sounds like the fabled Pace vanity starting to manifest itself in—"

"Hooey," countered Hildy. "It's a simple, and modest, assessment of the situation. If we can persuade one of the targets to leave the moon, we'll save at least—"

"Okay, give it a try, but be—"

"Careful. I know."

"Meantime, Steranko and I," said Jake, "will crash a party."

It wasn't much of a party.

In fact, it wasn't a party at all.

The chalet, its exterior rich with realwood gingerbread and colored tiles, nestled in a crater a quarter mile from its nearest neighbor and was not linked with the artificial day-night system that served most of the domed sectors of the moon. This sort of privacy was costly.

The place was dark.

"Where's all the gaiety?" asked Jake as he and Steranko approached the dark chalet from the rear.

"Maybe they've turned the lights down low to facilitate smooching."

"No noise either." They entered the flagstone courtyard behind the sprawling lodge.

"Sexual foolery doesn't make much noise, unless you draw a partner who is given to screams of glee and—"

"C'mon." Jake went trotting across the flagstones.

He hesitated a few seconds at the bottom of the real-wood steps leading to the rear door, then he went bounding quietly up.

The siphoner followed.

Jake slipped out a pocket scanning tool and ran it over the lock-alarm system. "This one isn't even as complex as the yard system we just fritzed," he said.

"I'm starting to agree with the proposition that nobody's home."

Crouching, Jake applied a tiny piklok to the lockbox. "I want to see what's inside anyway."

The door made a faint protesting moan before swinging open.

Jake waited on the threshold, listening. He put his entry tools into a pocket, drew out a short litestik and flicked it alive.

After sweeping the cone of illumination across the chalet's immense white kitchen, he stepped inside.

Steranko came after him, closing the door. Sniffing, he turned his own litestik on. "I was right about the caterers. See?" He played the beam over a butcher-block table piled high with real and sinfoods. A case of Chateau Discount Peppermint Champagne rested on the tile floor beneath the table.

Jake moved swiftly through the kitchen.

At the end of a long hall was a blind living room, showing nothing of the bleak moonscape outside.

He turned on a floating globelamp and doused his litestik. "Latterly plays the trombone," he said.

"Barely."

Jake kicked at the empty saxophone case that lay gaping on the yellow thermorug. "Must've had some of the group over."

"The atmosphere of this joint doesn't exactly soothe my . . . listen!"

Jake listened.

He heard a very faint moaning.

"Down that corridor yonder," he said, making his way to a half-open doorway.

At the end of a short, shadowy hallway another partially open door glowed pale orange.

Drawing his stungun, Jake started for it.

A very weak groan came drifting to him.

He saw the dark-haired girl first, lying on her back on the floor of the windowless bedroom.

She was the one who was moaning, in a feeble faraway way.

Jake's nose wrinkled and he hesitated in the opening. "Sleepgaz," he said. "And something else . . . some kind of mindwipe. Yeah, the same brand of stuff they used on me."

When he went in to kneel beside the unconscious girl, he spotted the other bodies on the far side of the wide floating hydrobed.

Three more of them, a plump red-haired young

woman, a lean black man and a blond youth in his low twenties. All unconscious on the fuzzy rug.

"Geez, is it a mass murder?" asked Steranko as he joined him.

"Nope, they're merely out cold, some kind of sleepgaz." Jake stood, went over to the other three. "None of them are members of the Big Bang gang."

The siphoner was rubbing his forehead. "I know this bimbo," he said, squatting beside the brunette. "Sure, she's the saxophone player in Latterly's group. Didn't recognize her right off without all the wacky makeup and goofy attire they all—"

"Tonight." Jake spun to face him. "They're going to do it tonight. Disguised as this bunch, with Latterly to help them. We've got to get over to—"

Slam! Bang!

The door to the room snapped shut, a heavy metal panel whizzed down over it.

In a dim corner of the room Woodrow the dummy suddenly sat up in a slingchair. "Guess again, sappo," he said.

CHAPTER 21

———————————————

Bonny Prince Freddy said, "Usually, Mrs. Pace, I do not become ... how you say *ardente* ..."

"Ardent?"

"No, more ... how you say *vigoroso* ... than that."

"Enflamed?"

"*Bom.*" He was a fat young man, packed into a two-piece gilt-trimmed soldiersuit. His hair was dark and curly, his moustache turned up at each end.

"Let me get to the reason for my dropping in on you in your private box here at—"

"You are ... how you say *bonita* ..."

"Pretty?"

"*Sim.* You are very pretty, even though you are a bit ... how you say *delgada* ..."

"Thin?"

The prince made another lunge at her. "Not quite. More ... how you say *descarnada* ..."

"Slender?" suggested Hildy, dodging him.

"Skinny." He leaped, with some grunting, over the padded seat she'd taken refuge behind. "But even though you are skinnier than the accepted standard in my native Portugal Annex, yet my eager ... how you say *coração* ..."

"Heart?" She straight-armed him, moved to the

148

edge of the box, which was along the right hand wall of Jazz Pavilion 2.

"*Sim*, my heart he beats with . . . how you say *luxuria* . . ." He made a charge at her, both arms outstretched.

"Lust?" She suggested, side-stepping and elbowing the prince in his plump side.

"Exactly, fair lady. I would like to go to . . . how you say *cama*..."

"Bed?"

"*Sim*, bed with you. It—"

"Pay attention, Prince Freddy." Hildy avoided him again, caught his arm and flipped him neatly into one of the box's four comfortable seats. "I came here not for romance—"

"But, fair lady, I sent away my bodyguards and my toadies, just so we could be . . . how you say—"

"Someone is going to kill you," she said. "Odd Jobs, Inc., that's my husband Jake and I, have reason to believe the Big Bang killers will make an attempt on you."

"*Quando?* Tonight you think?"

"Probably not tonight, yet sometime while you're on the moon."

He made a deflated sound, patted the seat beside him. "Tell me all you know."

Watchful, Hildy started to lower herself into the chair. "My husband already explained most of this to you this afternoon."

"Oh, *sim*, but I never pay much attention to men. A *rapariga* such as you, that is different. If I might rest my weary *carbeça* on your exciting lap while you recount in full the—"

"Nope." She dealt the wrist of the fat hand groping toward her a sharp chop. "You just sit there, behaving like the nobleman you're supposed to be, Prince

Freddy, and listen to me. I want you to pack up and depart from. . . ." Something on the stage attracted her attention and she didn't finish the sentence.

"If you were to help me pack, I might consider it. I have an impressive collection of pajamas I can model for you so that—"

"Hush for a minute." She punched his knee and leaned forward.

"Let's hear it for 'em," the silver-plated MC robot was telling the audience of nearly one thousand jazz enthusiasts below. "The group that finished third in the *Noise Magazine* jazz poll again this year. Here they come . . . Lafcadio Latterly and His Latter Day Saints!"

The five member band came marching toward the floating globe footlights. They gleamed and glistened and flashed, each wearing a sequin-splashed white robe and widespread golden wings. Their faces were painted gold and they wore standup wigs of fluttering silver hair.

"That saxophone player," said Hildy, frowning.

"He is Yardbird Kaminsky," said the prince. "When he was with Buddha and His Green Lamas his solo on *Jive At Five* was a . . . Ah, hello over there, dear old lady!" He'd noticed that Tilda Host was being installed in a box across the pavilion by Wranger and he raised up to wave and smile. "She's an old . . . how you say *cadella* . . ."

Hildy reached under the prince's wide rump. "That's not Yardbird Kaminsky under all that glitter."

"Ah, *rapariga*, you decide to play a little grabass, as you Americans say, after all—"

"You're sitting on the opera glasses."

Down on the wide stage Latterly was saying, "Greetings, gates, let's percolate. We got some cool sounds to lay on all you hepcats this yere evenin'. So don't be no ickies, chillun . . ."

Hildy fiddled with the focus button until she got herself a sharp closeup of the saxman. "Jesus H. Christ, it's Screwball Smith," she realized. "Yep, the lady next to him is Honey Chen."

"No, no, you know little of your native music, fair lady. That is Helen 'Fatlip' Lennon, the Queen of the Swing Cornet."

". . . get into a real groove this yere evenin', cats," Latterly was continuing. "We'uns is really gonna get cookin' for ya. Our first little ditty's a real gasseroo known as 'Hold That Tiger.' One-two-button-my-shoe. Three-four-let's-roar!"

The group began to play upon their vastly amplified instruments.

For a gang of assassins they weren't bad.

Hildy pulled Bonny Prince Freddy up on his booted feet. "C'mon, you're going to get over and warn Tilda Host. Then both of you are going to depart this concert," she told him. "I'm going to try to break up that bunch before—"

"But, sweet lady, I wish to hear the Latter Day Saints as they lay down some cool—"

"All you'll here is a loud bang." She tugged him to the box exit and out with her into a down-slanting corridor.

A royal bodyguard was stationed there. "Did you not score, your excellency?"

"This . . . how you say . . . ah, never mind. Mrs. Pace seems to think Mrs. Host and I are going to be killed unless we get out of here at once, José. I am coming around to her way of thinking. Therefore, let us make our way across to the box occupied by—"

"But, your highness, in this crush of jazz buffs it will take us many long minutes to wend our way—"

"Get going, quick." Hildy gave them both propelling shoves and went running on ahead down the ramp. "I'm going to have to halt these kids without benefit of Jake."

Too many people filled the corridor that led to the outside exit.

Hildy, elbowing and kneeing her way, wasn't moving fast enough. She pushed around wild-eyed youths in one-piece fansuits with *We Love Lafcadio* glolettered on the tunics, shoved through gaggles of media people and newsbots, finally reached the outside.

The easiest way to get backstage was to go around the pavilion, cutting through the grounds, and then into the stage entrance. Inside, the spurious group was still playing its rendition of "Tiger Rag."

Even more people out here in the artificial night. Multitudes of fans whose gloletter slogans declared their undying affection for Lafcadio Latterly, Zootz Zankowitz and a host of others.

"Dumb bitch!" observed a fat woman.

Hildy had collided with the fat vendor, causing her to lose her grip on five of the seven life-size Jazz Greats balloons she'd been hawking. The figures of two Lafcadio Latterlys, one Zootz Zankowitz and two Switchit McBernies, one for each sex stage, went swirling and flapping up into the air.

The vendor tried to grab Hildy. "You got to reimburse me, lady!"

"A bit later," promised Hildy as she side-armed the woman from her path.

She zigzagged through the throngs cluttering the path to the stage door. Up in the narrow opening two Pops with stunrods were urging the crowd back.

"But I have my Official Camp Followers Pass," a frail young blonde in a seethru parka was protesting.

"It's expired, honey," said a Pop scornfully.

Hildy kept up her push forward.

"No admittance, lady," a Pop told her when she was pressing against him at the head of the crowd.

She smiled sweetly, kneed him deftly in the groin and went dodging in around his doubling up body.

"Stop or I'll stun!" warned the other doorman.

Hildy skirted a wardrobe trunk, threw herself flat on the plazplanks of the backstage area.

Zizzzzzummmmmmmm!

"You oaf!" cried a green-haired young man who was passing with an armload of glocloth capes. "You've missed your target and stunned Chullunder Ghose, the head sitar player with Babu Billiken and his Himalayan Hillbillies."

"Glory be, sir, I swear I was aiming at that red-headed wench."

"Well, you better unstun him quickly or your toke will be in a sling for . . ."

Hildy, meantime, had gone skulking away between trunks and clothes racks and tumbles of electronic musical equipment, getting ever closer to the glare of the large half-oval stage.

She eased out her stungun.

It was going to require all five of them, far as she knew, to produce a Big Bang. By taking out at least a couple of them, she—"

"Gotcha, you slattern!"

It was one of the Pops and he'd come rushing out of the shadows to tackle her.

Hildy's stungun went spinning from her grasp.

It hit a backstage electric piano, bounced onto a wardrobe trunk and skidded under a beerpouch dispensing machine.

"Damn it, there's going to be an assassination." Hildy jabbed an elbow into the doorman's midsection.

"Oof . . . not while I've got hold of you . . . ooof . . . there ain't."

"Not by me, by them." She used her elbow again and broke free.

Out on the glaring stage the Latter Day Saints had concluded their first number. Great waves of shouting and applause came rushing up at them from the audience. With smiles on their golden faces, the five of them marched toward the floating footlights. They joined hands.

"That's how they do it!" cried Hildy. "Sure, they join hands and—"

"Now I have you, you crazed spalpeen!" Pop had tackled her once more, his arms tightening around her knees.

She gave him a chopping blow to the neck, kicked free and snatched away his stunrod as he went slumping to the hard floor.

"This damn thing doesn't have any range. I'm going to—"

Zzzzzzzummmmmmmmm!

Lafcadio Latterly stiffened, wings flapping twice, and went pitching over into the orchestra pit.

Zzzzzzzummmmmmmm!

Screwball Smith was next, letting go of his comrades and collapsing.

Somebody up in the catwalks over the stage was using a stunrifle. Two somebodies. Hildy glanced up and saw twin beams of yellow come knifing down.

Zzzzzzzummmmmmmmm!
Zzzzzzzummmmmmmm!

Honey Chen and Trina Twain, still holding hands, fell into each other, wings and robes swirling and tangling.

Derrick Thrasher was still standing. He shook a fist at the rafters, shouting, "I can get you alone, by concentr—"

Zzzzzzummmmmmmm!

He hit the stage with a feathery thump.

A moment later Jake came sliding down a dangling plaz rope.

The huge audience had long since jumped to its feet, angry, waving arms, shouting, screaming.

"Murder!"

"Assassins!"

"They've killed LL!"

"Get 'em!"

"Police!"

"Feds! Call the Feds!"

"Screw the cops!"

"Get your Lafcadio Latterly gloshirts here! Sure to be collectors' items!"

Jake, grinning, faced the outraged audience and held both hands high. "Ladies and gentlemen," he said into a dangling tokmike. "This is all part of the show. Nothing to be upset about. The management has asked me to assure you that—"

Thunk! Kathump!

Steranko hadn't dropped down from above quite as gracefully as Jake. He fell the last ten feet, landing smack in the electric drum set.

Riddydiddy! Blam! Kablang!

"Now they're wrecking his gear!"

"Killers!"

"Assassins!"

"To calm you all down after this exciting mock assassination," Jake went on, "I am going to play my famous jazz medley on the piano. Starting with Fats Waller and—"

"Boy, they'll lynch Jake if he tries that," murmured Hildy.

"Somebody'll lynch him. But it'll be the U.S. Government." Bullet Benton was standing beside her, a pleased snarl on his face. "I got here from the shuttle-port just in time to catch your sex-crazed husband in the act of murdering five innocent souls."

"Those innocent souls are the Big Bang killers," she said. "And none of them is dead. Jake only stunned them. Like this."

Zizzzzzummmmmm!

She used the borrowed stunrod to fell the burly Federal Police Agency cop.

Out on the stage Jake was seating himself at the piano. " 'The B-Flat Blues,' " he announced and commenced playing.

CHAPTER 22

⬥━━━◆━━━⬥

It came bawling out into the grey afternoon.

"Oh, I ain't no cyborg, baby, an' I ain't no cyborg's son. But I can slip you my spare part 'till the cyborg comes."

"Him again," said Jake.

"I ain't the downsize designer, mama, and I ain't. . . ."

"We may still need him," suggested Hildy, sliding out of their just-landed skycar.

"Why?"

"Bullet Benton, after he came to, was muttering something about pressing charges against me for assaulting an FPA agent."

"Fooey," observed Jake as he doubletimed up the ramp leading to their living room area. "The Zaboly Twins are speaking again and they won't let the Feds do anything to us."

"Bullet'll try," she said.

The freckled Lost Cause lawyer was again at Jake's white upright, banging at the keys as he sang. "Oh, I ain't the nuclear reactor repairman, baby, an' . . . Ah, the illustrious Paces return. Congrats."

"That why you broke in here?" Jake asked. "To congratulate us?"

"I still have the electrokey your dear, and incredibly amiable when compared to you, wife presented me," said John J. Pilgrim, facing them. "I did want to congratulate you and fill myself in on—"

"What's that stain on the carpet?"

"Ignore it," advised the lawyer. "Don't remind me of the sad fact that I spilled near a half liter of Chateau Discount Carbonated Pinot Noir with Extra Fluoride. One of my favo—"

"That gunk'll eat clean through the floor, you besotted shyster, and—"

"John, wouldn't you like to hear all the details about how Jake cleaned up the Big Bang case?" Hildy was holding Jake back from charging at the rumpled little attorney.

"I heard some of it, but—"

"Tell him, Jake. You did, after all, a brilliant job on this one."

Jake grinned. "I did, in fact. You were brilliant, too, Hildy. In your own way."

"It was you, Jake, who stopped them from blowing up Tilda Host and Bonny Prince Freddy." She arranged herself in a slingchair.

"True," admitted Jake.

Pilgrim said, "I heard you and that skinhead Steranko got yourselves locked up in a chalet. How'd you manage to—"

"That was not one of the more brilliant aspects of the investigation," said Jake, pacing some. "Matter of fact, we sort of got suckered into walking into what the gang figured would be a trap for us. They knew I had Steranko along, so they laid a false trail for him to pick up. They wanted us to believe nothing in the way of assassinations was planned for the first night of the festival. Actually they'd arranged for Latterly to appear and they stunned and mindwiped his real group. Trina left her snide dummy Woodrow behind, with a voxcaz stuffed into his inner workings, so he'd sit up and heckle us about being caught. She is fond of little nasty touches like that."

"How'd you get out?" asked Pilgrim while searching himself for a spare bottle.

"Well, I can't take all the credit for that."

"Would you care for a glass of spring water, John?" asked Hildy.

"Gung," he replied. "Go on with the yarn, Jake."

"There was a terminal for the home computer in the room they'd locked us up in," Jake said. "Steranko made friends with it and persuaded the damn thing to open up and let us go. He's got a way with machines."

"If not with people," added Hildy.

Pilgrim said, "How'd you sneak into the jazz pavilion?"

"Posed as musicians," replied Jake. "When I saw the real group out cold, I knew the gang planned to substitute and blow up somebody that night."

"I saw a vidtape of your piano medley, Pace, and I don't see how you get off criticizing my left hand," said the lawyer. "Wow, on the James P. Johnson segment you muffed—"

"I didn't muff a damn thing. And at least I—"

"Tell him about the confession," Hildy prompted.

After coughing into his hand, Jake said, "Derrick Thrasher gave the FPA and the Department of Security a full confession, which'll make the prosecution of the case a lot simpler."

"What prompted him to do a halfwit thing like that?"

"Foodopoly," said Jake. "They pulled assorted strings and the upshot is that if Derrick Thrasher tells all and helps the government put away the rest of the Novem bunch, he'll get off with six weeks at Murderers Home. After that—"

"But that whey-faced lad, working in a sinister symbiotic relationship with those other psychopaths, is responsible for the deaths of hundreds of people."

"After he gets out of the pokey," said Jake, "Derrick'll go to work for Foodopoly."

"Doing what? Slaughtering hogs for their—"

"He's got the Barrel implant in his skull," Jake said. "He can puff oats."

"He can also blow up people who—"

"Not alone." Jake shook his head. "To do that, as the class of '99 discovered, you need at least five of them. They have to be physically in contact with each other, joining hands, before they can concentrate and pool their psi powers to make an explosion where they want it. A big explosion, that is. Little ones Derrick can do alone."

"Suppose he builds new implants, based on the design of the one that's imbedded in his useless coco?" The frazzled lawyer was bouncing on the piano bench. "He can recruit a new group of five and we're back where we started."

"Jake did what he could," said Hildy. "He warned Secretary Strump about just such a possibility, but Foodopoly is damned powerful. All we can do is send back the darned bonus."

"What bonus?"

Jake said, "Bunny Thrasher sent us an additional $250,000 for locating Derrick for them. We turned that down."

Pilgrim blinked. "I thought you'd do anything for money, Pace."

"Almost anything," said Jake.